Contents

THE ICE-COLD CASE

1 Whose Lake Is It?

"Hey, it's cold back here," Frank Hardy's girlfriend, Callie Shaw, complained from the backseat of the Hardy brothers' van.

"We're almost there," Frank announced.

"Where does Sarah live anyway—Siberia?" Chet asked. Chet Morton, Phil Cohen, and Chet's sister, Iola, who was Joe Hardy's girlfriend, were also in back. Joe sat in the passenger seat next to Frank. They were heading to their friend Sarah Kwan's house for her birthday party.

Sarah Kwan lived in one of the large, handsome houses overlooking Pineview Lake. The road there snaked through the woods before it ended in a ring around the lakeshore. Hardly anyone ever used it at this time of year except local residents and ice fishermen.

The lake had frozen over at the end of January,

1

and now, in mid-February, the ice was thick enough for the fishermen to drive their trucks out and set up their fishing shanties. That meant, of course, that the ice was also perfect for skating.

As the van rounded the last slippery, snow-covered curve, the frozen lake spread before them.

"What a view," Callie said. "It's like a postcard."

At the end of the lake stood a small village of homemade ice-fishing shanties. The other end was being used for a game of hockey. In between, skaters raced, glided, and attempted figure-eights among other maneuvers.

"Race you across the lake," Frank said, challenging his brother.

"You're on," Joe said.

"Wow! Look at that," Frank said as he pulled into the Kwans' driveway.

Everyone strained to see out the front of the van. Sarah and her parents were putting the finishing touches on a snowman, but not just any ordinary snowman. This one was a frozen life-size sculpture of a real man sitting on a couch, watching television. And the whole scene was made of snow.

"I've never seen anything like it," Iola said as she peered over Joe's shoulder.

"Sarah's father is a sculptor," Callie explained.

"It figures!" Chet exclaimed.

Frank parked the van at the end of the driveway and hopped out.

Sarah waved and came over to greet them all. "I was worried you couldn't get through all this

2

snow," she said. Wearing a red parka and fluffy white ear muffs, she looked as if she belonged in a winter wonderland postcard, too.

The rest of the crew piled out of the van, wishing Sarah a happy birthday and stretching their legs. A few snowballs were thrown before they all trooped up the driveway to meet Sarah's parents.

"You must have been at this all morning," Callie said as she looked at the snow scene.

"Pretty much," Mrs. Kwan said.

"We actually started last night," Mr. Kwan added.

"This is my mom and dad," Sarah said. Her father looked very serious and had short graying hair. Her mother, however, was all smiles. Sarah introduced her friends.

When Mr. Kwan heard the name Hardy he came over and shook hands with Frank and Joe.

"There's something I want to talk to you about," Mr. Kwan said.

"Dad, please," Sarah said. "At least let them have some lunch first."

"Lunch isn't going anywhere," Mr. Kwan said. He turned his attention back to Frank and Joe. "Sarah has told me about your investigative skills."

"Just what do you think you're doing to these poor boys?" Mrs. Kwan asked as she came over. "They're here to have fun, not to listen to you."

"I'm just asking the Hardys if they know anything about the robberies around here," Mr. Kwan said.

"It's okay, Mrs. Kwan," Joe said. "Frank and I have solved quite a few crimes in and around Bayport."

"Some people collect stamps; we investigate crime," Frank added.

Mrs. Kwan looked skeptical. "Just remember, all of you, this is a party, not a crime stoppers' meeting."

Crime, however, tended to interest Frank more than parties. "What's the problem up here?" he asked Mr. Kwan.

"It's been going on for a few years now. Every winter someone's been breaking into houses around the lake and stealing things," Mr. Kwan explained. "The police aren't having much luck, and it's got a lot of us who live around here pretty nervous. I just thought if you boys heard or noticed anything while you were here—"

"Hiromi, come finish up here while I bring the hamburgers out to the grill," Mrs. Kwan called to her husband.

"I think I'd better get back to our work of art and let you boys go enjoy yourselves," Mr. Kwan said.

"Okay," Joe said. "We'll let you know if we pick up on anything."

Mr. Kwan went back to the snow sculpture, where Phil and Chet were admiring his work, and even more so, his tools. Mr. Kwan's tools were laid out precisely, like a surgeon's instruments. Spread around him were a snow shovel, kitchen knives, spoons, spatulas, and a large spray bottle.

"Looks like you've got a system," Phil said.

"The secret is to spray on water," Mr. Kwan

explained. "The cold air turns the snow to ice, which keeps the sculpture in shape."

"Hey, Phil," Chet said. "Let's make a snow-woman." Phil was game. He liked anything that required tools and skilled hands.

"We'll put her on a big recliner," Chet said as he started gathering snow.

Sarah led the others behind the house to the lake. "My dad checked the ice earlier. He says it's perfect for skating."

Joe paused to take in the view of the lake again. "This is a great place for a party."

"Nice place for a few robberies, too," Frank said.

"Ha, ha," Joe said, not really laughing.

"No joke—look at these houses," Frank said. Most of the houses were big, two or three stories tall, and well kept. They were surrounded by a good deal of land.

"Let's call Con Riley later and get the lowdown on those robberies," Frank said. Con Riley was an officer on the Bayport police force who had been helpful to them in the past. "But right now, I believe I have a race to win," Frank said.

"I wish I had brought my speed skates," Joe said as he looked over the broad, flat lake. "I didn't think the ice would be this smooth."

"Speed skates wouldn't help," Frank said. "I'd still beat you." Frank, at eighteen and six foot one, was a year older and an inch taller than his brother.

"In your dreams," Joe replied. He was younger and shorter, but Joe had a more athletic build, and he worked at keeping in shape.

5

"Okay, right now, you and me, on the ice," Frank said. They raced to the back of the van and grabbed their skates, which were laced on tightly in no time.

As they stood at the edge of the ice deciding their race course, they heard shouting from the far end of the lake.

"Is that still hockey they're playing over there?" Joe asked.

"Looks like tackle hockey to me," Frank said as he watched a central pile-up of bodies interrupt the wild game.

Sarah came over to them. "Sorry my dad was bugging you guys about the robberies. He's pretty freaked out about the whole thing and how the police haven't been able to catch the thief."

"No problem," Frank said. "We don't mind keeping our eyes and ears open. Right, Joe?" Frank nudged his brother, who was still focused on the hockey game.

"Isn't that Ray Nelson?" Joe pointed out a kid their age who, just at that moment, stuck out his hockey stick to trip an opponent.

"My father can't stand those guys," Sarah said. She winced as they watched Ray get flattened by another player.

"They're just a little rough," Joe said.

"A little rough?" Frank said. "Wasn't Ray suspended from school for fighting?"

"Okay, he's got a temper," Joe conceded. "But when we were on the football team together, he wasn't so bad."

"You were wearing pads," Frank said.

6

"Dad thinks Ray and his friends are the thieves," Sarah said.

Suddenly a shout came off the lake. "Get out of here!"

The action on the ice had moved. A swarm of hockey players was advancing on the fishermen's shanties.

"Do you think Ray and his friends are taking up ice fishing?" Joe asked with a laugh.

"Looks more like ice rioting to me," Frank replied.

A number of the fishermen were heading out to meet Ray and his hockey buddies. Some of them carried heavy steel rods called ice bars, which they used to test the ice and keep their ice holes from freezing over. At the moment, however, they looked more like weapons.

"We'd better check it out," Joe said.

As Frank and Joe skated out onto the lake, the shouting became more distinct. Ray was yelling at an older man. "Who said it was your lake anyway, Tuttle?"

"Get out of here, you punks," Ernie Tuttle shouted back. With his shock of white hair and the plaid wool coat he wore all the time, he was a fixture in Bayport. He had run Tuttle's Bait Shop—the only business along the lakeshore—for as long as anyone could remember.

"You, too!" Ernie shouted at Frank and Joe, who had skated right between the two groups. "You've got no business being on the lake."

"Chill out," Frank said. "We're not with them. What's everybody so angry about, anyway?"

Only a few feet separated the two sides, but the Hardys' presence seemed to calm them down a little.

Ray skated up to Joe, holding his hockey stick across his chest, ready to strike.

"We've got as much right to be on the lake as anybody," Ray said.

"Hey, what's the big deal?" Joe asked him.

While Joe tried to get Ray's side of the story, Frank saw Hank Green in the crowd of angry fishermen. Hank was a tall, slender man who always wore a red baseball cap that advertised his junkyard and fix-it shop, Green's Salvage, on the front. Joe and Frank's father, private detective Fenton Hardy, often called on Hank's expertise for cases involving cars. Hank would analyze wrecked cars to determine whether brake lines had been tampered with or engines had been sabotaged.

"Hank, remember me, Frank Hardy?" he asked as he skated up to him.

"Hey, Frank, how's your dad?" Hank asked. He reached out a gloved hand. Hank was so long and lanky, he looked as if he might blow away in the bitter wind.

They shook hands. "He's doing great," Frank said. "So, Hank, what's going on around here?"

"It never ends," Hank said with a sigh. "These kids skate around like crazy. They think it's great fun to scare away the fish. One of these days someone's going to get hurt. They'll knock over someone's shanty or fall through the ice."

"They're just fooling around," Frank offered.

"As far as I'm concerned, they can knock each other senseless on land," Hank said. "But if someone gets seriously hurt out here, the police will kick all of us off the ice."

"How about Ernie?" Frank asked. "He seems ready to blow."

"Can you imagine what'll happen to the bait shop if the parks commissioner declares the lake off-limits for the winter?" Hank replied.

While Frank and Hank had been talking, Ray began skating circles around Ernie, taunting him and waving his hockey stick at him.

"Come on, old man, kick me off the lake. Go ahead," Ray said. Two of Ray's friends who had been darting through the crowd of fishermen now skated directly toward Ernie with their hockey sticks raised.

Neither Frank nor Joe knew Ray's friends very well but had seen them hanging around town. Their names were John and Vinnie. They were a few years older and had dropped out of school. "How about it, old man?" Vinnie said, slapping Ernie on the back with the flat side of his stick.

Ernie pulled a hand ax from his tool belt. "All right, you punk. You asked for it," he shouted. But Vinnie had already skated out of Ernie's reach.

"Why don't you go back to the far side of the lake?" Joe calmly addressed Ray's friends.

Vinnie and John glowered at him. "Out of the way, Hardy," John said.

"Ernie, I know you've always been tough on your customers, but the ax is too much," Frank said.

This got a laugh from both the fishermen and the hockey players. Ray kept it up after the crowd had quieted.

"You think this is all a big joke, don't you, Ray Nelson," Ernie said as he put the ax back on his tool belt. "Well, I've seen you checking out the houses around here. I know what you've been doing."

"You'd better watch what you say, old man, or I'll shut you up for good," Ray threatened. He crouched low and picked up speed as he skated toward Ernie.

2 Unfriendly Warning

"What's it take to calm this guy down?" Frank asked his brother.

"Maybe he needs a nice trip," Joe said. He circled Frank once to gather speed and set off on an interception course. Just as Ray was bearing down on Ernie, Joe casually stuck his skate-shod foot out, closed his eyes, and braced himself for impact.

Instead of getting the expected jolt, he felt himself showered in ice chips at the same moment he heard police sirens. He opened his eyes to find Ray stopped, inches away from his face. Behind him, in the distance, three police cars were disgorging cops, who foolishly came charging onto the ice.

Both Joe and Ray found it hard to keep from laughing as the officers slipped and slid toward them.

The first officer on the scene was the Hardys' friend Con Riley.

"We got a call about a disturbance," Riley said as he surveyed the two groups.

"Tuttle thinks he owns the ice," Ray shouted from the group of skaters, where he had retreated.

"These punks are going to get someone killed," Ernie shouted back.

Then everyone else seemed to join in, shouting at once. Riley closed his eyes and shook his head. "One at a time," he yelled above the noise.

Frank and Joe skated up on either side of Riley.

"Don't tell me you're involved in this?" Riley said in disbelief.

"We would have been if you hadn't shown up," Frank said.

"So, tell me what's going on here, as if I didn't know." Officer Riley took Frank and Joe aside while the other officers stood between the two groups.

"Apparently the lake isn't big enough for fishing *and* hockey," Frank said.

"Yeah, yeah, I know," Riley said with a groan. "I've been out here at least a dozen times in the last three weeks."

Frank and Joe looked puzzled. "You don't want to hear what we have to say?" Joe asked.

"Talk all you want," Riley replied. "I just pulled you over here to wait for the chief to arrive. He told me to notify him the next time something like this happened and he'd come out himself. So, go ahead—talk if you want."

"See," Joe began, "the fishermen complain—"

"Hey," Frank interrupted. "Do you know those two guys?" He nodded in the direction of Tuttle's Bait Shop.

Two young men had come out the door and were heading toward the crowd on the lake. Ernie quickly went to talk to them. One was blond, about six feet tall, the other had dark hair and was a few inches shorter. Frank guessed they were in their twenties. The eyes of the whole crowd were on them as Ernie pointed Ray out to the two young men.

"They're Ernie's grandsons," Riley said. "Ernie introduced us. The tall one is Stu and the other is Neil. They come up from Maryland a few times a year to help with the shop."

At that moment, Chief of Police Ezra Collig arrived, and Riley hurried across the ice to meet him halfway. When the two policemen reached the crowd, Riley silenced everyone with a sharp whistle.

Collig addressed the gathered Bayport citizens. "Since you're all here, I want to know if anyone can tell me anything about the robbery this morning at the Anderson place."

Frank and Joe looked over the crowd to see if anyone would respond.

"I sure can," Ernie called out.

"Don't get involved." Stu tried to silence his grandfather.

"What do you have for me, Ernie?" Collig asked.

13

"I saw Ray Nelson snooping around there," Ernie said.

Ray heard this and exploded. "I warned you, old man. You'll pay for this, I swear." Ray was waving his hockey stick, and his face turned bright red.

"Now, take it easy, Ray," Collig said.

Joe skated over to Ray.

"Take it easy?" Ray shouted in disbelief. "That old jerk's been out to get me and my dad for years. Are you going to listen to his lies?"

"I'm going to hear what he has to say," Collig said. "When was this, Ernie?"

"All week, every night just about. And it wasn't the only place I saw him looking at, either," Ernie added.

"Are you willing to come down to the station and make a formal statement?" Collig asked.

"Sure I am. I'm not scared of these punks," Ernie said.

"Well, maybe you should be," Ray said.

"Why don't you arrest that bum," Ernie asked Collig.

Chief Collig rolled his eyes. "Ernie, it doesn't work that way. We'll get your statement and we'll get Ray to answer some questions." Collig waved an officer over. "Bring him in for questioning."

The officer made his way across the ice to Ray and his friends.

Ray turned to Joe. "Do something, Hardy. You know I'm no thief."

"Ray, they're just going to ask you some questions," Joe said.

The officer took Ray by the arm.

"C'mon, Joe. What about when I helped you find that kid who ran away, or when we caught Rob Dee stealing stuff from the gym lockers . . . ?"

"Ray, just don't make any trouble. I'll do what I can," Joe said. He didn't think of Ray as a close friend, but despite Ray's tough attitude, he had helped out the Hardys on a few cases.

The officer led Ray over to the police cars.

"Okay, Ernie, you, too," Collig said. "Do you need to close up shop before we go?"

"No, Stu and Neil can handle things," Ernie said. He followed the chief across the ice.

Frank, who was standing next to Stu and Neil, reached out his hand. "Frank Hardy. You're Stu and Neil?"

Stu shot Frank an angry glare.

"Hi. I'm Neil Tuttle."

Neil shook Frank's hand, but Stu just kept glaring.

"What was all that about seeing Ray checking out the places around here?" Frank asked.

"It's none of your business," Stu said coldly. He turned and walked away. Neil looked unsure for a moment but then followed his brother.

Joe skated over to Frank. "Ray wants me to help him," Joe said.

"Which side of this case are you working, Mr. Kwan's or Ray's?" Frank asked.

Chet had just skated over from Sarah Kwan's party. "Mr. Kwan was the one who called the police," Chet said. "He thought you guys were in trouble."

"We might have been in another few minutes," Frank said.

"Mr. Kwan is freaked out. He made everyone come inside until the police got here," Chet said.

"But we're a half mile away from the Kwans' house," Joe pointed out.

"Yeah, I mentioned that, but he said, 'Better safe than sorry,'" Chet reported.

"We'll be back in a few minutes," Frank said. "We just want to hang out awhile and see if we hear anything interesting."

"You guys are on the case already?" Chet asked.

"Yeah, we're just choosing sides," Frank said.

Chet looked confused. "What?"

"It's a joke," Joe said.

"Sure, whatever, Hardy," Chet said, shaking his head as he skated back to the party.

As the fishermen and the hockey players separated, Ray's friends Vinnie and John skated over to Stu and Neil, nearly hitting them with their hockey sticks, though making it look unintentional. Frank and Joe stayed close enough to hear their exchange.

"Keep an eye out for thin ice," Stu said.

"You're going to be sorry you messed with us," Vinnie snarled. Vinnie and John turned on the ice neatly and raced away.

"Ernie's grandsons sure have a way with people," Frank said to Joe as they watched Neil and Stu go back to the bait shop.

"Must be a family thing," Joe said, remembering Ernie swinging his ax at Ray. "And that makes me think I'd rather not meet Vinnie's and John's families."

"You want to go check out the Anderson house?" Frank suggested.

"I didn't get any lunch. I'd rather stop at the Kwans' first and see if there's any food left," Joe said.

Sarah, Iola, Callie, and the others were just coming back outside when Frank and Joe reached the far end of the lake. Mr. Kwan ran outside to get the last few burgers off the grill. They were little more than charcoal.

"Sorry, I got kind of sidetracked," Mr. Kwan said as Frank and Joe reached the house. "Let me put fresh ones on for you."

"Don't bother," Frank said.

"Yeah," Joe agreed. "Don't worry about it. We both like them well done."

"Thanks for calling the police," Frank said as Mr. Kwan brought them the overcooked burgers.

"Are you on the case?" Mr. Kwan asked.

"Just doing some legwork," Frank said.

"We're going to make a quick stopover at the Anderson place," Joe said as he wolfed down his burger. "Then I'm going down to the station to see how the questioning turns out."

After finishing their lunch and thanking the Kwans, Frank and Joe went around front to get their van. They saw Phil diligently working on the snow scene. He and Chet had made a snowwoman, and now Phil was trying to make a satellite dish out of snow, twigs, and ice behind the snow television.

"Hey, Phil, don't forget there's a party inside," Joe said as he got in the van.

"Life is not just a party. There must also be

17

satellite television," Phil said emphatically without looking up from his work.

"Wouldn't it be easier just to give them cable?" Frank asked Joe as they pulled the van out of the Kwans' driveway.

"Oh, I get it," Joe replied with a blank face. "Cable instead of a satellite dish. You're a real comedian, you know that, Frank?"

Frank answered with a jab to his brother's ribs.

The Anderson house was a large A-frame with a wall of windows facing the lake. A few police officers were there, still looking for clues, Frank figured. He and Joe looked around and found their friend Officer Riley.

"Do you have any leads yet?" Frank asked.

"If Ernie is telling the truth and not just venting his anger at the Nelsons, we may have already solved this one," Riley said.

"What did Ray mean that Ernie had it in for him and his dad?" Joe asked.

"Ernie and Ray's dad used to be business partners," Riley said. "The relationship didn't end well."

Riley was obviously not going to elaborate, so Frank changed the subject.

"How many houses have been hit?" Frank asked.

"All told, nearly two dozen over the last three years," Riley said.

"What's been stolen?" Frank hoped Riley wouldn't realize he was being grilled and clam up on them.

"Mostly silver and jewelry, watches, that kind of

thing," Riley said. "And none of the usual fencing operations got any of it. We've checked all the way into the city."

"You think they're stashing it, then," Frank continued.

"Either that or traveling a good way before they sell it," Riley said. "Do you think Ray is in on this?"

"I hope not," Joe said. "He can be a world-class jerk, but he did help us out on some cases. Deep down, I think he's okay."

"Let's hope so," Riley said.

Frank and Joe thanked Riley and then took a look around the Andersons' yard. With the footprints of so many police officers in the snow, it was impossible to identify where the robber might have stepped.

"Let's walk back to Sarah's," Joe said. "Maybe we'll see something new from that perspective."

"You know," Joe said after they'd gotten their footing on the smooth ice, "Ray couldn't have done it."

"Why not?" Frank asked.

"Didn't Riley say this has been going on for the last three years?" Joe asked.

"Yeah," Frank said.

"Ray went to live with his mother last year in Michigan," Joe said.

"Good point," Frank said. "Besides, do you think Ray would be stupid enough to antagonize everyone in the area and then rob their homes?"

"You'd think he'd keep a low profile," Joe said.

"So if it isn't Ray, who is doing it?" Frank asked.

"I guess that's what we've got to find out," Joe said.

When they returned to Sarah's house, they found everyone in the huge living room gathered around a roaring fire, drinking hot chocolate. Bundled up in the center of the crowd was Phil Cohen. Phil had been out working on the snow sculpture so long his fingers were nearly frozen.

"Who wants ice cream?" Mrs. Kwan asked as Frank and Joe came into the living room.

"I don't suppose you could serve it hot," Phil said with a groan.

Mr. Kwan took Frank and Joe aside. "So, did you guys find out anything?" he asked.

"Nothing definite," Joe said.

"The police are still looking for clues," Frank said.

"Leave them alone, dear," Mrs. Kwan said, handing them each bowls filled with chocolate, butter pecan, and mocha chip ice cream. "This is a party!"

But Joe wasn't about to let go of the investigation for the sake of a birthday party. Instead, he drew Mrs. Kwan into the discussion.

"What do you think about the break-ins, Mrs. Kwan? Have you seen anything?" Joe asked.

"Every time there's a robbery, the police ask us the same thing," Mrs. Kwan said. "And every time, I give the same answer: we didn't hear or see any cars pass by."

"And I don't think you could get a car by my house without me knowing about it," Mr. Kwan added. He put his ice cream down and put his arm around his wife's shoulder.

"Why is that?" Joe asked.

"Because the road is so near the house on the one side. We built too close, but it was either that or we would have had to blast out a boulder."

"There's so little traffic anyway," Mrs. Kwan said. "We moved here because it's so quiet—usually."

"So, are you boys going to stop this crime wave?" Mr. Kwan asked.

The Hardys were a little taken aback. They planned to do all they could, but they didn't want to promise the Kwans something they couldn't deliver.

"Well, we'll give it our best shot," Frank said with a faint smile.

"Not another word, Hiromi," said Mrs. Kwan. "We've already embarrassed the boys enough and kept them from the—"

Before Mrs. Kwan could finish her sentence, there was a loud crash from outside, instantly followed by screams.

3 Go Away!

They all ran outside and found shards of glass in the driveway surrounding the left side of the Hardys' van.

"Well, Frank, either someone's been practicing their slap shot on our van or they didn't like your parking job," Joe said as he opened the car door to survey the damage.

"Ow!" Joe yelped. He fell over a large rock with a piece of paper wrapped around it sitting in the middle of the passenger seat. "Hey, Frank," he said to his brother. "Do you remember seeing this rock here before the window broke?"

Frank gave his brother a good shove for acting so stupid. He bent over and picked up the rock. The paper was held on by a red rubber band, which Frank quickly removed. He unfolded the paper and read its message out loud: "'Hardys, stay off the lake. You're skating on thin ice.'"

"Well, we know one thing," Joe said, looking over Frank's shoulder. "Whoever did this has lousy handwriting."

Chet looked back and forth between the broken window and the Hardy brothers. "You guys make some new friends out there?"

"Yeah, Chet," Joe replied sarcastically. "We were getting a little tired of your company. . . . Just kidding!"

Fortunately, Chet was a longtime friend of the Hardys and was used to such abuse from them.

"I can't believe this," Mr. Kwan said as he walked over to inspect the van. "I'm calling the police."

"That's okay, Mr. Kwan," Frank said. "We have to stop by the station anyway. We'll report it. Meanwhile, do you have any plastic to cover this hole?"

By the time Frank, Joe, and Chet had finished duct-taping over the window with one of Mr. Kwan's tarps that he used in his sculpture studio, the party definitely seemed to be over.

The Kwans offered to drive everyone else home, so Frank and Joe could go straight to the police station.

"Let me know if you need my help," Chet told the brothers as he got into the Kwans' van.

"You're on, buddy," Frank said.

Chief Collig sat at his desk, reading what looked like interrogation reports as his secretary showed the two brothers into his office. "Frank and Joe Hardy—what can I do for you boys?"

"Someone threw this rock through the window of our van, along with this note," Frank said. He put the rock and the note on Collig's desk.

Chief Collig read the note. "Any idea who did this?"

"Well, it wasn't Ray, since he was here. We were hoping to catch him before he left. He may be able to help us, if he recognizes the handwriting," Frank said.

"You're in luck. He's still here," Collig said, "and will be for a while. He's in a heap of trouble."

"About that trouble," Joe said. "Ray wasn't even in Bayport last winter. He was with his mother in Michigan. So he couldn't have been involved in those robberies."

Collig nodded as if he'd heard all this before. "That was last year," he said gruffly. He paused. "Weren't you on the football team with Ray, Joe?"

"Yeah," Joe said.

"Look, I think it's very noble of you to help your teammate, but he's already admitted that he broke into one of the houses."

Joe looked dismayed. "What?"

"He said he and some friends went into Ari Brown's place, and it was robbed about two weeks ago," Collig said.

"He admitted he was involved?" Frank asked.

"Not exactly," Collig explained. "He said they went in on a dare. But the fact is he admitted to breaking into the house."

24

"Can we talk to him?" Joe asked.

"Be my guest," Collig said, standing up.

"Oh, and could we get a photocopy of that note?" Frank asked. "I imagine you'd like the original, but a copy may help us out."

"Oh, all right." Chief Collig picked up the note and led Frank and Joe out of his office. They stopped off at a copy machine, which looked and sounded like a dying dinosaur, but the chief got a decent copy from it.

"Thanks, Chief," Frank remembered to say.

The brothers followed Chief Collig to a cell in the back of the building.

Ray was sitting on a bunk with his head in his hands.

"You've got visitors, Ray," Collig said, then turned around and walked off.

Ray looked up and saw Frank and Joe on the other side of the steel bars. "Are you guys going to get me out of here?" he asked.

"We'll see what we can do . . ." Frank began.

"But first we need to talk." Joe finished his brother's sentence for him.

"Ray, someone threw a rock through our van window with a note attached," Frank informed him, watching for any signs of whether he was surprised by the news.

"The note warned us to stay off the lake," Joe said.

"That's what that jerk Tuttle is always yelling at me," Ray said. "Are you getting me out or what?"

"We mentioned to Chief Collig that you weren't

in Bayport last year so you couldn't have done those robberies," Joe said, ignoring Ray's question.

"So you believe I'm innocent?" Ray asked.

"I'm not sure I'd go so far as to call you innocent, but I'm not convinced you're a burglar," Joe said.

"So what did Collig tell you?" Ray asked. He stood up and walked over to the bars that separated him from freedom.

"He said you admitted to breaking into the Brown place," Joe said.

"It was a dare, that's all. You know, raid the fridge and hang out. We just thought it would be a laugh," Ray said.

"A laugh?" Joe echoed.

"I know. It sounds pretty stupid to me, too, right now," Ray admitted.

Collig suddenly reappeared with a set of keys jangling from a large ring.

"Okay, Ray, you're going home," Collig said.

"That's great. Thanks, guys," he said to Frank and Joe.

"We can't take credit for this," Frank said.

"Oh, no," Ray said, then groaned. "My dad isn't here, is he?"

"Nope. When I called him, he said you could rot in that cell for all he cared," Collig said.

From the look on Ray's face, Frank realized that Collig wasn't kidding.

"We just got a call that someone broke into another house. It's safe to say you didn't do it, since you were here," Collig said.

"So, you're letting me go?" Ray asked.

"We may have more questions for you later. Maybe your friends here can give you a ride home," Collig said as he unlocked the cell.

"No problem," Frank said. He had wanted to talk to Ray without the police around.

When they reached the van, Ray asked if the thrown rock had hurt anyone. He looked at the broken window. "They really got you."

"Yeah, and we'd really like to send whoever did it a thank-you note," Frank said.

Ray climbed into the back of the van. "What is all this stuff?" he asked, looking at the equipment Frank and Joe kept there.

"We never know what we're going to need when we're on a case," Joe said. "It's tools mostly and some winter gear."

Frank got in behind the wheel and pulled the copy of the note from his pocket. "Take a look at this, Ray. Do you recognize the handwriting?"

Ray took the note and examined it by the light from the dashboard.

"Can't say I do, but I probably wouldn't even if my best friend had written it," Ray said.

The night was getting colder, and the roads were becoming more treacherous. Frank and Joe kept two fifty-pound bags of cement over the back tire wells to give the van more traction in slippery conditions. But even with this added weight, Frank had to be very careful as he drove.

"So what do you think is the story behind these robberies?" Frank asked Ray as they made their way across town.

27

"How should I know?" Ray replied stiffly.

"Ray, Chief Collig is going to pin this on you and your friends," Frank said. "We're trying to help you. The least you can do is cooperate with us."

"How could he pin it on me? I was in jail during the last robbery."

"Which makes it look like your friends pulled it to make sure Collig would let you go," Frank said. "By admitting to breaking and entering, you've become his prime suspect."

"I didn't have anything to do with any robberies. It's probably that nut Tuttle," Ray said.

"So when Ernie saw you checking out the Anderson house, you were just going to break in for the fun of it?" Joe asked.

"I wasn't checking it out—at least not the way he thinks," Ray said. "You ever see houses like that? That's the way I want to live someday."

Frank and Joe knew what he meant. Sarah lived in one of the smaller houses by the lake, and it was huge. The Anderson place was a mansion.

"It's not a crime to admire a nice house," Ray said.

"It is if you go in and look around without an invitation," Joe reminded him.

"So I've been told," Ray replied. "But I didn't have anything to do with robbing those places, and I don't think any of my friends did, either."

"Then help us with something," Frank said. "I'd like to see samples of their handwriting to see if any of them wrote this note."

"I'm not going to spy on my friends," Ray said.

"No one is asking you to," Joe said. "We just want to know if one of them threw the rock through our window."

"Besides, Ray, if Chief Collig decides to blame you for the robberies, we may be the only real friends you have," Frank added.

"Did Vinnie and John come to the station?" Joe asked.

Ray was quiet for a moment. "I'm sure they were busy," he said defensively.

"That much I guessed," Joe said.

"Look, I made a mistake going into the Brown place," Ray admitted. "But as for the rest of it, it's just Ernie trying to get back at my old man by blaming me for something I didn't do."

"What's with Ernie and your old man?" Joe asked.

"They used to be partners. The bait shop and all the land around it belonged to both of them, fifty-fifty," Ray said with an edge to his voice. "But my dad had some hard times when he and my mom got divorced."

"So what happened?" Joe asked.

"My dad asked for a loan, but Ernie wouldn't help him out. My dad even suggested they sell a few acres of land, but Ernie wouldn't do it. Finally, when my dad was nearly desperate, Ernie bought him out for next to nothing. My old man didn't have a choice. They've hated each other ever since."

"Isn't your place around here somewhere?" Frank asked as he reached a secluded road on the far end of town.

"Yeah, on the right, under the big tree," Ray said, pointing to a huge tree that reflected the van's headlights on snow-covered limbs.

Frank slowed the van and concentrated on rounding the icy curve into the driveway.

"Some place," Joe said as he looked at the beat-up cars and fallen trees that lined the path to the small house. There was a board over one of the windows, and the roof was sagging.

"Yeah, my dad calls it home," Ray said. "But if Ernie had helped him out years ago, we'd be living in one of those lakefront mansions now."

As Frank brought the van to a stop, a man wearing a camouflage jacket stepped out from behind an old beat-up Volvo. He raised a shotgun to his eye, released the safety, and aimed directly at them through the windshield.

4 Fishing for Clues

"Dad, it's okay; it's me," Ray shouted to the man with the shotgun.

"That's your father?" Frank asked.

"Yeah, and you caught him on a good day," Ray said as he got out of the van.

"What kind of trouble are you in now?" Mr. Nelson shouted. He lowered the gun.

"I didn't do anything," Ray said.

"The police don't take your kid to the station unless he did something," Mr. Nelson shouted, his face red.

Frank and Joe got out of the van slowly so they wouldn't alarm Mr. Nelson.

"It's Ernie Tuttle's fault," Ray said.

"Tuttle? What did he do?" Mr. Nelson demanded.

31

"Why don't we go inside and warm up," Ray said as he led the way into the house.

"Tuttle is the most low-down cheat in Bayport," Mr. Nelson said.

"Ray told us about your business with him," Joe said. He climbed the broken front steps, careful to step over the rotted boards.

"You'd think *I* was the one who ripped *him* off!" Mr. Nelson said as he put down his gun and flopped into a ratty old lounger.

Ray waved for Frank and Joe to sit on the couch, where a big, mangy-looking retriever was asleep. The dog made no effort to move when Ray tried to shoo him away. Frank decided to stand. Joe looked around the room and did the same.

"So, Mr. Nelson," Frank said, "have you heard about the robberies out by the lake?"

"Tuttle's doing it," Mr. Nelson said, the angry edge rising in his voice.

"Why would he bother?" Joe said. "I thought he was rich with all that land."

"Just to be ornery," Mr. Nelson grumbled. Then he turned his attention to his son. "Why were you in the police station?"

"Ernie said he saw me casing the houses," Ray replied sheepishly.

Mr. Nelson got up and slammed his fist into the wall, cracking the plaster. "That good-for-nothing lowlife," he shouted. "Isn't it enough he ripped me off and wrecked my life? I'll show him," he said, going for his gun.

Frank stepped in front of him to keep the gun out

of reach. "I'm sure the police are questioning everybody," he said.

"What's it got to do with you, anyway?" Mr. Nelson snarled at Frank.

"Dad, they're trying to help me," Ray said.

"We don't think Ray was involved in the robberies and we want to help him prove it," Joe added.

"This is between me and Tuttle," Mr. Nelson said.

Frank didn't budge, keeping Mr. Nelson from his gun. "Mr. Nelson, the police will pin this on Ray unless we find the real robbers."

"Dad, it's not like we can afford to hire anybody," Ray reminded him.

"Well, all right," Mr. Nelson said. "But if Tuttle does anything else to my son, I swear I'll blow his head off."

"We'll keep that in mind," Joe said.

As they walked back to the van, Ray came out. "Thanks for your help in there. By the way," he said as Frank started the motor, "you should really fix that window."

"So we've heard," Frank said.

Frank backed the van out of the driveway. "Was it just me or was that a weird scene?" he said to Joe.

"No joke. I'll take a cold van and icy roads any day," Joe said, "over the inside of that house another minute."

"Any ideas?" Frank asked Joe as he steered the van back to town.

"I guess we should get Phil to fix the heat," Joe said.

"I mean about the robberies," Frank said.

"What do you think of Mr. Nelson's theory?" Joe asked.

"That Ernie's behind the robberies?" Frank asked. "Not much. Doesn't make any sense."

"I agree. Ernie doesn't seem to need the money, and there's nothing to be gained by scaring people away from the lake," Joe said as they drove through the deserted downtown.

"But what's with Ernie's attitude? It was bad enough when he was being mean to customers on his own. Now he's got his grandsons to back him up," Frank said.

"The short one, Neil, didn't seem so bad," Joe said.

"His brother, Stu, just reeks of loser," Frank said as they pulled into their driveway.

It was quite late, and the house was quiet. Frank and Joe tiptoed upstairs to check the messages on their answering machine. Joe flipped the play button and immediately recognized Officer Riley's voice: "Just thought you should know there was a suspicious fire at Tuttle's. Come by in the morning and I'll walk you through it."

Frank and Joe drove to Tuttle's early Sunday morning to inspect the fire damage. When they arrived, Officer Riley was at the scene, along with Ernie's grandsons, Stu and Neil.

The fire had destroyed a storage shed a dozen yards from the main building, which housed the bait shop and Ernie's home. All that remained of the shed were charred embers. The snow all around had melted from the heat of the fire. Now the mud was turning to solid, frozen ground.

As Frank walked over from the van, he caught the acrid scent of burned plastic.

"Frank and Joe Hardy, I think you've met Stu and Neil Tuttle," Officer Riley said.

"Yesterday," Frank said. They shook hands all around. Frank noticed that Stu wasn't as cold to them as he'd been the day before.

"So, what have you got?" Joe asked.

"Arson," Stu Tuttle said before Riley could respond.

"Well, it doesn't look like an accident," Riley said. "See over there?" He pointed to the charred remains of a gasoline can. "Someone doused the place and lit it up."

"We don't sell cans like that," Stu said.

"Anybody see anything?" Joe asked.

"We were in back with our grandfather when we saw the flames," Stu said.

"We tried to put it out, but the hose was frozen and the shed went up so fast," Neil added.

Stu shot Neil an angry look.

"What was in the shed?" Frank asked.

"Mostly summer stuff—rafts, buckets, inner tubes, that kind of thing," Stu said.

Just then a few fishermen walked into the shop.

"Excuse us," Stu said as he and Neil went to help their customers. Joe noticed that Neil, the shorter of the two, seemed to be scared of his brother, Stu.

"What do you know about those two?" Frank asked Riley when Stu and Neil were in the shop.

"Just what I told you yesterday. Their story checks out with Ernie."

"Where is Ernie?" Frank asked.

"Fishing," Riley said.

"Really?" Frank said. "With all this going on?"

Joe walked into the pile of rubble and began slowly picking over the charred remains. "Did anyone else poke through this stuff?"

"Our forensic people and the fire department," Riley said.

"What about Ernie and his grandsons?" Frank asked.

"They looked to see if they could salvage anything," Riley said. "We've already looked for shoe prints, but we haven't found anything."

"Thanks, Officer Riley. We really appreciate your calling us about this," Frank said.

"You should be careful. It was bad enough when we just had the robberies. Now we've got your broken window and arson, too," Riley said. He scanned the frozen lake. "Things are a lot less peaceful out here than they look."

"So, what now?" Joe asked Frank.

"I think we need to talk to Ernie," Frank said as he led the way down the steep embankment to the lake. The ice was nearly a foot thick at that end of the lake, which made it safe for the ice fishermen.

Joe marveled at the elaborate shanties, some with television antennas on top.

"Who's cooking?" Frank asked as he smelled the faint brown-sugary aroma of baked beans.

"Bacon and coffee," Joe said as he inhaled. "This is my kind of sport."

"You're not kidding. Frying bacon and television? I had no idea ice fishing was so strenuous," Frank said with a chuckle.

"Look at this," Joe said as he pointed to names and local addresses painted on the doors of each cabin.

"I guess that's in case your shanty walks off, it can find its way home," Frank said, and laughed.

Ernie's shanty was smaller than most of the others and showed definite signs of age. The plywood walls were peeling apart, and the tar paper stapled onto the roof was fading from exposure to the sun.

Frank knocked on the flimsy door. "Ernie, it's Frank and Joe Hardy."

"Get in here and stop scaring the fish," Ernie replied gruffly.

Joe opened the door. The shanty was packed with equipment, buckets, rags, reels, nylon fishing line, and lots of used coffee cups. Joe noticed what looked like a large motorized drill with a corkscrew blade nearly a foot across.

Ernie was bundled up, sitting on an old chair that had stuffing coming out of the arms. He was holding a short fishing pole over a small trapdoor in the floor. The fishing line disappeared down into a hole in the ice.

"Close the door," Ernie snapped, his eyes fixed on the little red-and-white float bobbing in the icy water.

Frank and Joe squeezed in.

"We wanted to ask you about the fire," Frank said.

"Ray Nelson did it. He was paying me back for accusing him of being a thief," Ernie said.

"We were with Ray last night. He couldn't have done it," Joe said.

"So you're on his side now?" Ernie asked.

"We're not on anybody's side," Joe said. "We're trying to find out who broke our van window. It might be the same person who burned your shed."

"When did you notice the fire?" Frank asked.

"Around ten-thirty. We were playing cards, me and Stu and Neil."

"Did you see anybody? Any cars or anything?" Joe asked.

Ernie looked up for a moment. "Don't you think that if I saw someone burning my place down I would have stopped them?"

Then Ernie gave a little cry as the float on his fishing line bobbed under the surface.

"Got something?" Joe asked.

"Shh," Ernie hissed.

Frank and Joe watched as Ernie let out more line. Then he gave the line a quick jerk.

"Aw, shoot," Ernie mumbled. "Lost him, thanks to you."

"Ernie, do you have any idea who else might have set the fire?" Frank asked.

"I already told you. It was just lucky there wasn't anything expensive in there," he said as he reeled in his line.

"Nothing valuable was lost?" Frank asked.

"No. Stu found a leak in the shed roof yesterday, so we moved all the good stuff into the shop."

"Was the shed insured?" Joe asked.

"Nope."

"Ernie, what's this thing?" Joe asked as he pointed to the big drill-like object.

"It's a power auger. Drills holes through ice two feet thick," Ernie said.

"Why does everyone paint their names on the shanties?" Frank asked.

"It's the law, that's why," Ernie said. "If anything happens, they know who to call," Ernie said. "Now, you leaving or fishing?"

Frank and Joe left Ernie and went searching for Hank Green to see if he could help replace the broken window in their van.

Hank didn't have a fancy ice shed. He carried his gear on a sled and sat on an upturned bucket while he fished, bundled up against the cold. When Frank and Joe found him, he was looking very cold.

"How are they biting?" Joe asked.

"You'd have to find someone who's had a nibble to answer that," Hank said. "I'm thinking I should do something smart, like go home."

"Funny you should mention that," Frank said. "Do you think you might have a driver's-side window for a van like ours?"

"Someone broke ours last night. Sent us a note with a rock," Joe explained.

"Strange stuff is going on," Hank said. "But it's a good excuse to go warm up."

They helped Hank pack his gear and then followed his green pickup truck to the junkyard a mile from the lake. It was surrounded by a chain-link fence with slats running through it to keep the ugly disarray of old cars from view.

It didn't take Hank long to find the remains of a van similar to the Hardys'.

"Looks like we're in luck," Hank said as he removed the inner door panel to expose the window mechanism.

While they were removing the window, the phone rang. It was hooked to a loud bell on a pole so Hank could hear it anywhere on the lot.

"I'll be back," he said as he ran inside.

Frank and Joe were lifting the window out when Hank returned with a worried look on his face.

"What's up?" Frank asked.

"What's up is that phone call. Someone just warned me that I'd be in trouble if I helped you."

5 Let's Get Him

"Did you recognize the voice?" Joe asked Hank.

"No, but I'm not worried," Hank said. "What are they going to do? Turn my junk into junk?"

"Someone did torch Tuttle's storage shed," Frank said.

"That's terrible," Hank said.

"Do you have any idea who it could be?" Joe asked.

"I hope it's somebody I don't know, 'cause I just don't want to think someone I know could do this," Hank said.

"What do we owe you for the window?" Frank asked Hank when they finished.

"It's on me," Hank said. "Think of it as my contribution to your investigation."

Frank and Joe thanked Hank and then plotted their next move.

"I'm still thinking about what Mr. Kwan said yesterday about not hearing any cars drive by," Joe said.

"What about it?" Frank asked.

"Whoever is doing this doesn't need to drive by the Kwans' because they must already be in the area. How else would they know where we left the van the other day or know to call Hank's just now?" Joe said.

"You're assuming that our broken window, Hank's call, and the robberies are connected," Frank said.

"Let's go see just how hard it is to get a car by the Kwans' house," Joe suggested.

They drove to the lake, taking careful note of the narrow road in front of the Kwans' house. It went over a rise from which they could look into the upper windows at the side of the house.

"The headlights must shine right in the windows," Frank said.

Frank hit the brakes as they swerved down the little hill into a sharp turn between the Kwans' property and a huge boulder. Then he hit the gas to climb the short rise on the far side of the curve.

"It would be hard to miss all this noise," Frank said as he swung the van into the Kwans' driveway.

"Maybe snow muffles the sound," Joe said.

Even before they stopped the van, Sarah came out to the driveway.

"I heard you come up," she said.

"Well, that supports my theory," Frank said.

Frank went inside while Joe drove the van back and forth in front of the house. Without even looking out the window, Frank could hear the van every time, even when Joe tried to sneak by at about two miles an hour. They tried again, using Mrs. Kwan's quieter sedan. They could hear it almost as clearly as the van.

When Mr. Kwan got home from shopping, Frank and Joe told him about their test.

"I tried to tell the police, but they insisted that I slept through it," Mr. Kwan said.

"Believe me," Mrs. Kwan said, "he doesn't sleep through anything these days."

"Thanks for your help," Frank said as he and Joe put on their coats. "We're going to take a look around."

They drove farther down the road and parked the van away from the houses in a small clearing by the edge of the lake. The sun was setting, and the evening chill was coming on.

"Can you believe how early it gets dark?" Joe asked.

"Why couldn't we be doing this in the summer?" Frank grumbled as he put on his heavy winter gear, including spikes for his boots so he wouldn't slip on the ice.

They went to the woods and picked up branches about six feet long and a few inches around, breaking off the twigs and loose bark to make sturdy walking sticks. They used them to tap on the ice to make sure it was solid before stepping on it.

"You're right about one thing," Frank said. "Whoever's doing all this isn't coming by car. They either walk through the woods or they're already in the area by nightfall."

43

"If they walk through the woods, it could be anybody," Joe said.

"What do you think about the Tuttles?" Frank asked as he looked over at the bait shop.

"Seems a little too lucky that they took all the expensive stuff out of the shed before the fire," Joe said.

"You're right about that," Frank agreed. "But I'm still stumped on a motive for Ernie."

"I know, but it would explain why the Kwans aren't seeing any cars," Joe said. "And the fire could have been a diversion to throw us off."

"Maybe they're just trying to make Ray and his friends look guilty," Frank said.

They walked around the lake for nearly an hour, taking note of which houses had lights on and which were dark.

Joe stopped and stared at a large house belonging to a friend of their father. "Frank, check out Lindsay Dixon's place." Through an upper window, he saw a man carrying a television.

"Isn't Lindsay in Europe?" Frank said.

"That's what I thought. So who's the guy with the TV?" Joe said.

"What kind of idiot robs a house with all the lights on?" Frank asked.

"Let's get him!" Joe said.

"Let's call the cops first. He could be armed," Frank said.

"And let him get away?" Joe said as he began running toward Dixon's house.

They climbed onto the large deck behind the

44

house. Then Joe used a thin metal tool he carried with him to unlock the sliding glass door.

"Ready?" Joe whispered.

They pushed the sliding door open. Joe slipped into the house and Frank followed quickly behind.

They heard heavy footsteps above them as they made their way to the stairway. Joe pointed to a door under the stairs. "Basement?" he whispered.

Frank opened the door to the basement and saw the fuse box at the top of the stairs. Joe nodded. Frank slowly opened the fuse box, but the metal door squeaked. Frank froze, waiting for a reaction from above. They heard nothing. Frank reached into the fuse box and turned off the main circuit, sending the house into complete darkness.

"What the . . ." came a voice from upstairs.

"Get back," Frank whispered to Joe.

The man who had been carrying the TV came lumbering down the stairs while Frank and Joe hid just out of sight. When he reached the bottom step, Joe dove and tackled him. They rolled across the floor as the guy tried to push Joe off. He got an arm free and reached for Joe's throat. Joe struggled to hold him, but the guy was big—at least six feet tall—and had an athletic build. Frank guessed he was in his thirties.

Frank ran over and got his arm around the guy's neck in a choke hold.

"Give it up, buddy," Frank shouted.

The man finally stopped struggling. Frank held him pinned to the floor.

"Who are you?" Frank demanded. "What are you doing here?"

"What are *you* doing here?" he shouted back.

"Where were you going with that television?" Joe asked.

"Take it—you can have it. Just leave me out of this," the guy said.

"We know about the robberies," Joe said.

"And we want to know what else you took," Frank added.

"I didn't take anything; I'm house-sitting."

"Why were you carrying the TV?" Joe asked.

"I was moving the big TV to my bedroom," the guy said.

"Whose house is this?" Frank asked.

"Lindsay Dixon. He's in Italy for the winter. My name's Doug Lang."

Frank waved at Joe to let Lang up. "We're investigating the robberies around here and we saw you," Frank explained.

"How do I know *you're* not the robbers?" Lang said indignantly.

"How do we know you're really the house sitter?" Joe replied.

"Because I'm telling you I am," Lang said.

Joe reluctantly let Lang up off the floor.

"Anyone might know where Dixon is," Joe said. "Can you prove you're house-sitting?"

"Lindsay offered me the place so I could paint in peace," Lang said.

Lang led them upstairs, though Frank and Joe were careful to be sure he wasn't leading them up to an accomplice. Lang showed them his clothes in the closet. "And how do I know you guys are on the level?"

"Call the police and ask," Frank told him. "We're Frank and Joe Hardy."

Lang went to the phone and dialed.

"Yeah, my name's Doug Lang," he said into the phone. "I'm house-sitting at Lindsay Dixon's house. . . . Do you know Frank and Joe Hardy?"

Frank and Joe watched Lang's expression change.

"So they *are* investigators. Why am I asking? Because they just jumped me," Lang explained. "No, no I don't want to file a complaint. What I want is to be let alone."

"Can I talk to him?" Frank asked.

Lang handed Frank the phone.

"Hi, this is Frank Hardy. Is Chief Collig there, please?" Frank smiled at Lang. A moment later Collig got on the phone.

"Chief Collig? It's Frank Hardy here. Do you know if Lindsay Dixon has a house sitter in his place?" Frank asked.

Collig told Frank he had a letter from Dixon about Lang.

Frank took a deep breath as he handed the phone back to Lang. "We owe you an apology."

Lang hung up the phone.

"We're really sorry," Joe said.

"Will you please get out of here and leave me alone?" Lang said.

"Sure, but if you see or hear anything, will you let us know?" Joe asked.

"I think I'll just call the cops," Lang said as he ushered them to the door.

When Frank and Joe got back onto the lake, they

47

picked up their walking sticks and proceeded to tap their way around the rest of the lake.

"I think we really bonded with him there," Joe said, then laughed.

"I'm not going to hold my breath waiting for a dinner invitation," Frank said.

"You'd think with all that's going on around here, he'd be more appreciative that we were trying to protect him," Joe grumbled.

"Maybe he doesn't know what's been going on," Frank said.

"Or maybe he knows exactly what's going on," Joe said pointedly.

"Hey, just because we mugged him and he doesn't see the value in it doesn't make him the bad guy," Frank said.

"Just something to consider," Joe said.

The night was getting colder, and the wind was picking up. They spent another half hour completing the circle of the lake but saw nothing out of the ordinary.

Suddenly the quiet of the night was sliced by the roar of a chain saw.

"Who's cutting wood at this hour?" Frank asked.

Joe looked back to the spot where they had parked the van, a few hundred yards away. "Sounds like it's coming from near the van."

When they reached the van, the noise had stopped and there was no sign of anyone.

"Everything looks okay," Frank said.

"Let's head home before someone breaks another window," Joe said as they climbed into the van.

Frank put the van in gear and got back on the road.

Suddenly there was a flash as the gleaming headlights caught a large tree falling across the road just a few feet in front of them.

"Look out!" Joe shouted.

Frank slammed on the brakes and turned the wheel sharply as the van skidded into the path of the falling tree.

6 Shattered Glass

The brakes screeched, and the van lurched to a stop.

"I've never seen a tree with moves like that," Joe said as he grabbed a flashlight from the glove compartment. He hopped out and ran to the base of the fallen tree. He could see sawdust on the ice surrounding the stump. "It's been cut all right," he called to Frank. "Almost all the way through."

Frank came over to Joe, who was now shining the light into the dark forest.

"See anything?" Frank asked.

"No," Joe said. "But they were smart. The ground is all icy here, so they wouldn't leave any tracks."

They were standing in a low part of the forest that in warmer weather would be a swampy bog.

Now the ground all around them was mottled ice with fallen branches and twigs sticking out.

"And the woods aren't very thick, either," Frank added. "They could've pushed the tree over and made a break for it. Whoever did it is long gone by now."

They went back to the van and saw that Frank had brought it to a stop only a few inches from the tree.

"We'd better move that tree before anyone else drives into it," Frank said.

The tree was too heavy for them to drag across the road, so they took a rope and tied the tree to their van. Joe stood by the tree and signaled to Frank as he backed the van up, dragging the tree across the road. Then they used their walking sticks as levers to push the heavy trunk off the road so no one else would hit it.

"Who's trying to tell us something?" Frank asked as they got into the van.

"It could have been Ray's friends," Joe suggested as Frank drove cautiously down the road.

"They could have broken our window," Frank conceded. "And they have plenty of reason to be angry at Tuttle."

"And they could have staged that last robbery to get Ray out of jail," Joe added.

"True enough. But none of them live around here," Frank said. "So, how do they get here?"

"You mean without driving by the Kwans'?" Joe asked.

"Right. I'm thinking it's someone right here at

the lake. How else would they have known to call and threaten Hank if they hadn't seen us with him?" Frank said.

Joe thought for a moment. "I didn't like that Lang guy," he said. "He seemed to have an attitude."

"I agree," Frank said. "But then we didn't make much of a first impression ourselves."

"No, I suppose not," Joe said.

"And he found out we were looking into the robberies only tonight," Frank said.

"So he's not the one who broke our window," Joe said.

"And he wouldn't have a reason to burn down Tuttle's shed," Frank said.

"Unless he's another dissatisfied customer of Tuttle's Bait Shop. You know their motto—Service with a Vengeance," Joe said.

Frank laughed. "Another possibility."

"Ernie and his grandsons wouldn't have to get here by car," Joe said. "And they know the area pretty well."

"So they burned the shed to throw us off?" Frank asked.

"It's kind of suspicious that they cleared out all the valuable stuff the day before the fire," Joe said. "And they'd have seen us with Hank, too."

"Maybe we should swing by Hank's and make sure he's all right," Frank said as they reached the main road.

"Do you think he's in danger?" Joe asked.

"We nearly caught a falling tree, didn't we?" Frank said.

He pulled the van onto the main road and quickly turned it toward Hank's junkyard. They reached Hank's in minutes.

Floodlights came on as they pulled into the driveway. When Frank stopped the engine, they heard Hank's dog barking like crazy. A moment later Hank came out. He looked exhausted and was wearing a parka over his pajamas.

"Hey, Hank, everything all right around here?" Joe called out to him.

"Joe Hardy, is that you?" Hank asked. Hank's breath was visible in the cold night air.

"Yeah, and Frank, too. We went out by the lake and someone threw a tree at us. We thought we'd better stop by and see if you were okay. Especially since you got that phone call."

Hank came over to the van. Frank had never seen Hank without his red hat. His bald head looked almost soft with so many wrinkles.

"It's been noisy out here tonight. Red's going nuts," Hank said, pointing to his dog, who was now running around the wrecked hulks of cars stacked along the fence.

"What do you think he's so excited about?" Frank asked.

"Oh, it's just deer or raccoons or something," Hank said.

"Do you mind if we take a look around?" Frank asked.

"I'll join you," Hank said. "It's not like I'm

getting any sleep with that dog barking his head off."

Frank and Joe got out of the van, each carrying a flashlight. Hank went back to his trailer and got another flashlight and then turned off the lights flooding the junkyard.

"I probably scared 'em away with the lights and the dog," Hank said as the three of them quietly walked down the rows of cars. Now that Hank was on the prowl, Red stopped barking and followed closely behind.

"So you didn't come outside when Red was barking?" Frank asked.

"No, I figured it was either nothing or Red was scaring them away, so I didn't bother," Hank said.

They walked through the junkyard with their flashlights off.

"What did you mean someone threw a tree at you?" Hank asked.

Joe explained about the chain saw and the tree falling across the road.

"Sounds like someone's trying to tell you something," Hank said.

"That's what we thought," Frank said. "It occurred to us that it might be someone coming through the woods."

"You mean past my place?" Hank asked.

"That's one possibility," Joe said.

"Shh," Frank said as he crouched low. "Hear that?"

"What is it?" Joe whispered.

They listened to the biting chill of the wind and

then heard a light shuffling sound from the other side of the fence.

"Probably a raccoon," Hank whispered.

"We'll see," Frank whispered back. "Joe, give me a leg up."

Frank and Joe crept to the side of the fence. Joe put down his flashlight and cupped his hands so Frank could use them for a step. Frank jumped up and grabbed the top of the fence with one hand while Joe hoisted him up. Frank looked over the edge of the fence and shined his flashlight into the woods.

"See anything?" Joe whispered.

"No," Frank said as he continued to look into the woods. "Wait . . . I see footprints."

He trained his light to the base of a large tree, where footprints led away from the fence.

"Hank, did you get much snow here last night?" he called down.

"Just an inch or so," Hank said.

"Then these footprints are fresh," Frank said. "Let me down."

"Let's follow them," Joe said.

Frank and Joe ran to the entrance of the junkyard and around the fence, with Hank and Red following after.

"Hank, you may want to stay here, just in case," Frank said.

"I'm coming with you," Hank said.

"But it may just be a trick to get us away from here," Frank said.

"Why would anyone do that?" Hank asked.

"Someone's already torched Tuttle's place," Frank reminded him.

That was all Hank needed to hear. He grabbed Red by the collar and led him back to his trailer while the Hardys ran around to the back of the junkyard and picked up the tracks Frank had seen over the fence.

"This way," Joe said as he shined his flashlight at the fresh tracks.

They followed the tracks deeper into the woods.

"Do you feel like you're being watched?" Frank whispered to Joe.

"This might be a trap," Joe said.

They turned off their flashlights so they'd be less visible and followed the tracks by the moonlight. The moon was nearly full, and the light reflected off the snowy ground, giving the forest an eerie glow. As they trekked on, they saw that they were headed back to the lake.

"What do you think?" Joe whispered.

"They cut the tree and came over here to see Hank," Frank said.

"Maybe they didn't count on the dog," Joe suggested.

"Or us," Frank said.

They hiked on and saw the shiny ice of the lake through the forest.

"So we're back here again," Joe said.

"Yeah, and I'll bet we lose the tracks once we reach the ice," Frank said.

They came out of the woods a few feet from the lake. Just as Frank suspected, the tracks ended right at the edge of the lake.

"Lost 'em," Joe said in frustration.

They stood by the edge of the lake, looking for any sign of movement. Suddenly the silence was broken and a loud crash of shattering glass pierced the night.

7 Follow the Shadows

"Sounds like it was over there," Frank said as he pointed toward the large A-frame they had been in earlier that evening.

"Dixon's place?" Joe said.

As they ran toward Dixon's, Frank saw two shadowy figures in the moonlight skating across the lake. They were dragging a box the size of a footlocker behind them. Frank nudged his brother. "Joe, check this out."

Joe saw the two shadows disappear into the gathering of shanties at Tuttle's end of the lake. "I'll go after them."

"Let's scope out Dixon's first," Frank said. "They could be armed."

When Frank and Joe reached Dixon's, they saw that the huge sliding glass door leading to the deck had been shattered. Joe scrambled up to the deck.

"Look out for glass; it's all over the deck," he said to Frank, who was climbing up after him.

They stepped through the broken glass and entered the house, where they found the house sitter, Doug Lang, lying facedown on the floor of the living room. His head was bleeding and he was unconscious. Frank got down on his knees and felt Lang's neck, checking for a pulse.

"He's out cold. Looks like someone hit him right across the forehead," Frank said as he looked at Lang's wound.

Joe went to the phone to call the police. He was careful to pick it up by the earpiece so he wouldn't disturb any fingerprints that might be on the handle. "We just found the house sitter at Dixon's place. He's been hurt. Looks like someone hit him with a bat or something."

After Joe hung up the phone, he went back to the terrace and looked over the lake while Frank stayed with Lang.

"We should go after those guys," Joe said as he looked at the shanties.

"Let's wait for the police," Frank said. "Lang's bleeding a lot. I don't want to leave him."

While they waited for the police, Joe looked around the house. Other than the shattered window, there didn't seem to be anything amiss. But until Lang regained consciousness, they couldn't be sure that nothing was stolen.

"I'll call Hank and ask him to bring the van over," Joe said.

After he called Hank, Joe began pacing in front of the window like a trapped animal.

"You realize that every minute we wait, the perpetrator is getting farther away," Joe said.

"Joe, we'll get out there in a few minutes," Frank said. "By the way, did you notice something funny about the broken window?"

"You mean that the broken glass is outside?" Joe responded.

"Yeah, that window was broken by someone leaving the house, not coming in," Frank said.

"So they broke in and Lang walked in on them," Joe said.

"He probably got hit before he knew what was happening," Frank suggested.

Then they heard Hank calling to them from outside. "Hey, Frank? Joe?"

Joe went to the front door and let Hank in.

"Whoa, what happened here?" Hank asked.

"Pretty much what you see. Someone smashed the window and hit Lang," Joe explained.

Soon the police arrived with an ambulance. The paramedics took Lang's vital signs.

"Is he going to be all right?" Frank asked.

"Yeah. He's lucky the wound isn't deep," one of the paramedics said as they placed Lang on a stretcher and prepared to take him out to the ambulance.

Frank and Joe told the police about their evening. After the police took down their statements, Frank and Joe went out toward the lake.

Officer Riley was looking around the backyard with a flashlight. "We've got a set of footprints here."

"We saw two guys on the lake," Joe said.

"It looks to me like there was only one guy," Riley said as he pointed to the tracks that led from the house to the road and back. "He must have left the car around here somewhere."

"I don't think they came by car," Frank said. "We followed someone through the woods from Hank's place."

"How do you explain these footprints?" Riley asked.

"I'm not sure yet, but I don't believe for a minute that whoever's doing all this drove here tonight," Frank said.

"Maybe someone wants you to think they're coming from the road," Joe suggested. "We would have heard them or seen the car," Joe said, recalling the quiet darkness that was shattered along with Dixon's window.

"Well, I've seen enough," Riley said. "It's too cold for me out here anyway." Riley went back inside as Hank came out.

Joe shined his flashlight on the ground between the back of the house and the lake and saw two parallel ruts in the snow.

"I'm going to get a ride home from Riley," Hank called to them.

"Hank, come here a minute," Joe said. "Look at this. What are these tracks?"

"Could be a sled box," Hank said.

"A sled box?" Joe asked.

"Yeah, like the one I have, the tackle box on sled runners," Hank explained.

"That's it, then; it was those two guys," Joe said.

"Let's go have a look," Frank said.

But rather than walk out onto the ice, they walked into the woods until they were sure they weren't visible from the lake. Then they walked parallel to the shore, a hundred yards through the woods, to an outcrop of rock. Crouching low behind the rocks, they had a clear view of the lake.

"It's awfully quiet," Joe whispered as he looked over the lake.

"Too quiet," Frank whispered back.

"Frank," Joe whispered, "do you have the feeling we're being watched?"

"Yeah, pretty much ever since we left Hank's," Frank agreed.

They watched the stillness of the ice for nearly an hour before they saw something moving.

"Joe, look over there, by the shanties," Frank whispered.

"It's them. They're on skates," Joe whispered back.

"Let's go," Frank said.

"They'll see us on the ice," Joe said.

"Walk slowly. We'll look less threatening," Frank said as they made their way across the lake.

"You think they'll make a break for it?" Joe asked as they approached the shanty village.

"I doubt it. They know we'd see which way they go," Frank said. "Besides, it could be someone perfectly innocent," he reminded his brother.

"Could be," Joe said, though he didn't think it was likely.

They hid next to the first shanty they came to.

"Do you think they saw us coming?" Joe whispered.

"I'm sure of it," Frank said.

They crouched low and crept around the shanty and found themselves at the end of a row of shanties, each about twenty feet away from the next. The shanties were all closed up with no lights on except for one at the far end, closest to the shore, which had a faint white glow coming from the windows. Frank pointed to it.

Joe took the hint and they made their way, one shanty at a time up the row. Suddenly they saw two shadows by the shanty at the far end.

"Hello there!" Frank said as he ran toward them.

Joe held back for a moment to make sure they didn't both walk into a trap.

Frank reached the shanty at the head of the row and found the door swinging open. He waved for Joe to stay back while he looked in.

Joe saw a shadow, but before he could react, he was knocked off his feet by someone in black wielding a steel bar. The bar whacked into Joe's side, sending him sprawling to the ice. Joe tried to call out, but the pain in his side kept him from breathing. He tried to fight, but he couldn't get his footing on the slick ice.

The attacker grabbed his coat and flung him into the shanty with his brother. The door to the shanty slammed shut, and they heard someone attach a padlock to the door. Frank tried to open the door, but it wouldn't budge.

Joe lay on the floor of the cabin and tried to catch his breath.

"Are you all right?" Frank asked.

"Yeah. I just got the wind knocked out of me," Joe said finally as he got to his feet.

"Looks like someone was expecting us," Frank said.

"Cozy in here, isn't it?" Joe said as he tried to open the door.

"A little too cozy," Frank said as he tried to open a window. Both the small windows were sealed shut. "We're trapped."

"What about the floor?" Joe asked.

They reached down to the little trapdoors the fishermen used to lower their lines through. Like the windows, the trapdoors were nailed shut.

"Looks like we're here until the fishermen show up in the morning," Joe said.

"I don't think so," Frank said. "The heater's on. It's going to burn up all the oxygen if we don't shut it off."

The gas-fired camp stove was burning with a whitish glow. Frank tried to find a switch to turn it off. "Someone's broken the switch. I can't turn it off."

"So we suffocate or freeze," Joe said. "But either way—we're trapped!"

8 Squeeze Play

"There must be *something* we can do," Frank said, rummaging through the fishing gear.

"Maybe we can drill our way out," Joe said as he picked up the sharp corkscrew blade of a power auger. "I'm sure this would cut through the plywood of the shack."

"The door's our best bet," Frank said as he helped Joe lift the auger.

They each took one of the auger's handles. It was designed to be used vertically, so it was difficult to manage on its side.

The motor started just like a lawn mower, with a sharp yank on a cord. Joe gave the rope a good strong pull. The engine made a coughing sound but didn't start.

Joe pulled the cord again, and this time the motor spewed exhaust and kicked in. It was so loud that Frank thought they would go deaf by the time they got the door open.

Joe tapped Frank on the shoulder to let him know he was ready. They tilted the machine up and thrust the big drill bit into the door. Wood chips went flying and the whole cabin shook. Frank and Joe leaned heavily into the auger handles, then stumbled as the auger broke through the door. They yanked the auger back in as Joe cut the engine.

"At least now we'll have some air until we get out of here," Frank said. He reached through the hole and felt the padlock on the door.

"We can pry the lock off," Joe said. He searched through the gear and found a six-foot-long steel ice bar weighing nearly twenty pounds.

"Try this," Joe said as he handed it to Frank.

Frank passed the ice bar through the hole and used it as a lever against the hinged shackle. He gave it a few short pushes.

"Let me try," Joe said.

Joe was a bit stronger than his brother, and at a time like this, Frank wasn't going to let his pride get in the way. He held on to the bar while Joe reached out to take hold of it.

With one quick push, Joe rammed the steel bar, and they heard a loud crack as the lock popped off and the door swung open.

"We're out of here," Joe said as he dove out into the refreshing chill of the night air.

"Not a moment too soon," Frank agreed. "Anyone out here?"

"They're long gone," Joe said as his eyes scanned the lake. Joe read the name on the door. "Do you think this guy Paul Rizzo knows something?"

"I don't know," Frank said. He closed what was left of the door. "We're going to have to fix this."

"Let's first see if the van's still in one piece," Joe said.

They made their way across the lake to where they had left the van.

"Unbelievable. No one touched it," Frank said.

"Let's get home before someone does," Joe said.

After school the next day, Frank and Joe went back to the lake with a small piece of wood to patch the door to Rizzo's shanty.

"Well, if it isn't the Hardy boys," Ernie said as he came across the ice from the bait shop. "Stu said he saw you down here, but I didn't think you boys knew Rizzo."

"We don't, really," Joe said.

"Then what are you doing to his shanty?"

"Just a little patch job," Frank said as he nailed the wood over the hole in the door.

"Ernie, did you see anyone on the lake last night?" Joe asked.

"Me? No, I stayed in. But you should ask Stu and Neil. They were out fishing most of the night. Not that they caught anything. Sometimes I don't know what they do out here," he added with a shake of his head.

"Interesting," Frank said. "We'll have to go see them later."

"First, you have some work to do," Ernie said. "Your patch job sure looks bad. I think you'd better replace the whole door." With that, he turned and walked to his shanty.

When he was out of earshot, Joe turned to Frank, "Stu and Neil were out all night fishing and they didn't catch a thing?"

"Well, they may have caught us," Frank said.

"Do you think Ray's friends are off the hook?" Joe said.

"I don't know, but where are they now? I thought they played hockey every day," Frank said.

"Maybe they're avoiding the scene of the crime," Joe said as he looked over the lake.

"We should go see Ray and find out if he's avoiding *us*," Frank said. He finished nailing the patch to the door and stood back to survey his work. "I think Ernie's right. We'd better replace the whole door," he said.

"First, let's go see if Stu and Neil have anything to say about last night," Joe said.

They walked up to the bait shop. Stu was behind the counter, and Neil was arranging some reels on a rack nearby.

"Hey, remember us? Frank and Joe Hardy," Frank said.

Neil said hello, but Stu just fixed them with a sullen stare.

"Ernie told us you guys were out fishing last night," Joe said.

"So?" Stu said.

"We were out on the lake last night, too, and we

68

ran into a little trouble. I was wondering if you saw anything," Frank said.

Stu looked at Neil before speaking. "If I tell you something, you promise to keep it to yourselves?"

"Sure," Frank said.

"Well, Ernie's not too cool about us hanging out and partying in town, so we always tell him we're going fishing," Stu said.

Stu looked over at Neil, who nodded his agreement. "We go out like we're going to fish, but then we hitch a ride into town," Neil said.

"Where do you guys hang out?" Joe asked.

"Different places," Stu said. "It's the only fun we get when we come to visit our grandfather. If you get us busted, you'll be sorry."

"No problem," Frank said as he and Joe turned to go.

They loaded their tools back into the van and headed over to Ray's house.

"They sure got nervous when we asked about where they go," Joe said.

"Besides, how many places are open that late?" Joe asked.

"Not too many," Frank said. "Let's check them out later."

"You know what, Frank?" Joe said. "It really is cold in here."

"So I've heard. We'll get Phil to rig something," Frank suggested.

"Drive in slowly," Joe said when they reached Ray's driveway. "I don't want to surprise Mr. Nelson again."

"You and me both," Frank said.

Ray was in the garage with his friends Vinnie and John. They were working on Ray's truck.

"Check that out," Joe said as he looked at the jacked-up suspension and oversize tires.

"He works on it so much that I don't think I've ever seen it on the road," Frank said.

Before Ray saw Frank and Joe, Vinnie came over. "What do you want?" he said with an edge to his voice.

"Hey, it's the hotshot Hardy boys," John called from the garage.

Frank noticed the torn look on Ray's face. Ray needed their help, but he didn't seem to want his friends to know it.

"We're here to see Ray," Frank said calmly, eager not to be drawn into a fight.

"Joe Hardy, why don't you let me wipe you out in some no-rules hockey?" Vinnie taunted.

Frank wasn't in the mood for a game of dare, but he knew Joe wouldn't shrink from a challenge.

"Name the time and place, and you're on," Joe said as he stood his ground before Vinnie.

"Today, at the lake. Two-on-two. No rules," Vinnie said.

"First to score three goals wins," John added.

"I'll be referee," Ray said as he wiped the motor oil off his hands. "Come inside," Ray said. "I'll be back in a minute," he called to Vinnie and John as he led Frank and Joe into the house.

Ray's bedroom had posters of supersize trucks and motorcycles on the walls.

"I thought of something that might help you

guys," Ray said. He reached into a drawer and pulled out a card with a picture of a monster truck.

"My friends sent it to me at Christmas last year when I was in Michigan. They all signed it."

"Thanks," Frank said.

"Do you happen to know where Vinnie and John were last night, around eleven?" Joe asked. "We got jumped at the lake."

"They work the night shift at Burger World," Ray said.

"Don't mention anything. We don't want to tip them off," Frank said.

"They're not the ones," Ray said vehemently.

"We're just narrowing down the list, Ray," Frank said as they headed back outside.

"I'm going to wipe your hide all over the ice later," Vinnie called when he saw Frank and Joe heading to the van. "They're going to need a snow shovel to get you home," he added.

"Don't count on it," Joe replied.

Frank took his brother's arm and pulled him along. "We'll settle this on the lake."

"Be there in a half hour," John shouted as Frank pulled the van out of the driveway.

"Unless you're too chicken to show up," Joe shouted back.

"Save it for the ice," Frank said to Joe. He pulled Ray's postcard from his pocket. "We'll check it when we get home. We've got to get our skates, anyway."

When they compared the card to the note, they were disappointed to find that none of the handwriting matched.

"Just because Vinnie and John's writing doesn't match," Joe said, studying the card, "doesn't mean they didn't do it."

"Just because they like to give you a hard time doesn't mean they threw the rock through our window," Frank countered.

"Just because they didn't send the rock through our window doesn't mean they aren't committing the robberies," Joe reminded his brother. "So let's go nail them at hockey."

They swung by their house, grabbed their gear, and drove out to the lake. When they arrived, Vinnie and John were already on the ice, slapping a puck back and forth. Vinnie and John were good hockey players, Frank noticed.

"Come on, let's get this game started," Joe said.

"Wait up." Frank took his brother's arm. "Let's watch for a sec."

"Why?" Joe asked.

"Watch Vinnie's left side," Frank said. "He's weak on the left."

Sure enough, when John shot the puck to Vinnie's left, Vinnie nearly missed it.

"Good observation," Joe said as Frank finished lacing up his skates.

Frank and Joe skated onto the ice where Vinnie and John were playing. Ray had set up two rocks to indicate goals at either end of a rink he had outlined with a few sticks.

"Hey, Joe, we have a cheering section," Frank said as he pointed to the Kwans' house. Sarah and her father were standing by the lake, watching them.

"They're probably wondering what we're doing with these guys," Joe said with a chuckle.

"Hey, you gonna play hockey or what?" Ray called to Frank and Joe.

Joe and Vinnie came together for the face-off. Ray counted to three and dropped the puck. Before Joe could even reach for it, John yanked Joe's foot from behind with his stick, sending Joe sprawling to the ice. Vinnie knocked the puck away and raced down the ice toward the goal. Frank jumped over Joe and chased after Vinnie, but John skated right at him and knocked him down.

"Score!" Vinnie shouted.

"What about the hooking?" Joe asked Ray as he got to his feet.

"No rules—remember?" Ray said.

"So that's how you want to play," Joe said.

Frank knew that Joe was up for this kind of game, but he didn't like the idea that it could escalate into a brawl.

Joe was ready for the next face-off. At the count of two, he lunged forward and knocked Vinnie off balance. When the puck fell, Joe flicked it over to Frank. Frank took off down the ice, expecting John to trip him with his stick at any moment.

"Watch your head, Frank," Joe called out.

Sensing John coming up behind him, Frank pulled the puck close and came to a stop, crouching low with the long handle of his stick poking out a few feet behind him. John was too close to stop. His chest rammed into the handle of Frank's stick, and his feet shot out from under him.

Frank skated off to the far end of the rink and

73

gently tapped the puck in for a goal. From the distance, the Kwans cheered.

"One all," Ray called out.

It wasn't long before the score was tied at two. Frank had scored by pounding away at Vinnie's weakness on the left. Vinnie and John scored when Ray dropped the puck at one instead of three at the face-off.

At the last face-off, John got the puck to Vinnie. Frank crossed in front of Vinnie so that when Vinnie tried to work the puck on his left side, Frank stole it and fired the puck down the ice to Joe. Joe was racing to break away from John, and for a moment he thought he might be in the clear.

"Joe, look out!" Frank shouted.

Joe realized that Vinnie and John were coming right at him from opposite sides. Neither of them seemed to be paying attention to the puck. They seemed more eager to cream Joe.

They skated as fast as they could, heads down, with the handles of their sticks pointing at Joe like bayonets.

9 Sore Losers

Joe waited to the last second before passing the puck to Frank. In the same motion, he lunged headfirst onto the ice.

"Look out!" John shouted, but it was too late. He and Vinnie were going too fast to stop. They crashed into each other with such force that they bounced backward onto the ice.

Frank was the only one left standing. He skated casually to the goal, then stopped before gently tapping the puck through.

"Score," he said quietly.

"The Hardys win," Ray announced.

Joe got up and waved to the Kwans, who were applauding the victory.

Frank skated over to Joe as Vinnie and John rubbed their bruises.

"So, who's going to wipe who off the ice?" Joe said to Vinnie.

"You won. No big deal," Vinnie said. "Sorry to cut short your victory, but we've got to get to work."

"What time is it, anyway?" John asked.

Ray checked his watch. "It's nearly five."

"You like working the night shift?" Frank asked.

"Would you like flipping burgers from six to two in the morning?" John said before he and Vinnie skated back to Ray's truck.

"Good game," Joe shouted as he and Frank skated to their van. "Good for us at least," he added under his breath.

"We should check the schedule at Burger World," Frank said, hopping into the driver's seat. "If they were working when Lang was attacked, I'd say they're in the clear."

"Let's go see if Hank can tell us something about the guy who owns that shanty we were locked in last night," Joe said.

At Green's Salvage, Red greeted them, barking and wagging his tail. Hank came out of his office to see what Red was so excited about.

"Hey there—how're you doing?" Hank asked as Frank and Joe got out of the van.

"We just played some hockey, so we're feeling pretty good," Joe said, still enjoying the win over Vinnie and John.

"Speak for yourself, Joe. I'm starting to feel pretty sore," Frank said. He rubbed his side where John had rammed into him.

"How about some hot cider?" Hank said. "Come inside."

They went into Hank's cluttered trailer and managed to pull three chairs up to Hank's table.

"I can't believe you ever find anything in here," Frank said as he moved an air filter off a chair.

"Oh, I know where everything is," Hank said. "Unless someone else comes in and moves something. Then I'm in big trouble," he added, with a chuckle.

Hank took a pot off a little electric hot plate and poured three cups of steaming cider. Frank and Joe wrapped their cold hands around the hot mugs.

"So, what brings you here?" Hank asked as he sat back in his chair.

"We had a run-in with someone on the lake last night after you left," Frank said.

"They locked us in one of the shanties," Joe added.

"Whoever it was must have been expecting us. The shanty was all sealed up," Frank said.

"Whose shanty was it?" Hank asked.

"Paul Rizzo's," Frank said.

"There's no way that Rizzo is involved," Hank said without a hint of hesitation. "Little guy, maybe seventy-five years old. He used to run the diner out near the highway with his brother. He comes to the lake only on weekends now," Hank said.

"Rizzo didn't know about any of this, I'll bet," Joe said.

"That's right. He barely knows which shack is his," Hank said with a chuckle. "He's a nice guy, but he isn't much of a fisherman."

"Does he have any family who might use the shack?" Frank asked.

"I think he's got two daughters who live in Florida. His brother still runs the diner. I tell you, Rizzo isn't the type to be mixed up in anything," Hank said.

"But everyone knows he's on the lake only on weekends?" Joe asked.

Frank knew what Joe was thinking. "So, anyone who's out there with any regularity would know the shanty is empty most of the time?"

"Yup," Hank said as he poured them more steaming cider.

"And unless I miss my guess, they've been keeping a pretty close watch on us every time we're out there," Frank said.

"Hank, did you see anybody hitchhiking around here last night?" Joe asked.

"In this weather? It's way too cold," Hank said.

"It does sound crazy," Frank said.

"Sure does. Red would have barked his fool head off if someone had walked by, and he didn't," Hank said. "So, who do you think it is?"

"Well, we don't want to jump to any conclusions, but I'm beginning to think we should be spending more time around Tuttle's Bait Shop," Frank said.

"Ernie?" Hank said. "That's ridiculous."

"It's got to be someone who can watch the lake pretty much all the time," Frank said.

"Do you know much about Ernie's grandsons?" Joe asked.

Hank sat back in his chair. "No, I don't know them very well," he admitted. "They stay pretty much to themselves."

"It's only a theory," Frank said.

"I'll keep my mouth shut," Hank said. "You can count on me."

"Thanks a lot, Hank. And don't take any chances. Whoever's out there hurt Lang pretty bad," Frank said as he stood up.

"Don't you worry, Red and I will be safe," Hank said as he held the door for them.

"I'm so hungry, I could eat a . . . burger," Joe said as they went back to the van.

"Burger World it is, then," Frank said.

When Frank pulled the van out onto the main road, he noticed headlights in the rearview mirror.

"Joe, keep an eye on those lights behind us," Frank said.

Joe leaned over so he could see out the passenger-side mirror. "How long have they been back there?"

"I first noticed them when we pulled out of Hank's. I think they were waiting for us."

"Who do you suppose it is?" Joe asked.

"Well, Lang's in the hospital, and Vinnie and John are supposed to be at work. Unless I miss my guess, there's only one other choice."

"Stu and Neil Tuttle?" Joe asked.

"Bingo," Frank said.

When Frank pulled into the Burger World parking lot, the lights behind them disappeared. They

79

waited in the van to see if anyone drove by, but no one did.

"The driver must have cut the lights when he saw us pull in here," Frank said. "Why don't you wait with the van while I go check out Vinnie and John's schedules. Honk if there's trouble."

"While you're at it, how about a cheeseburger and some fries?" Joe said.

Frank went inside, where he saw Vinnie and John in their Burger World uniforms, flipping burgers in the back. They spotted Frank and made faces at him, still not happy about having lost the hockey game.

Frank ordered some food from the girl at the counter.

"Were Vinnie and John working last night?" Frank asked.

"Who are you? Their parole officer or something?" the girl asked.

"Just a friend," Frank said.

Vinnie came up to the counter.

"This guy wants to know if you were here last night," the girl said to Vinnie.

"What's it to you, Hardy?" Vinnie asked.

"It's about what's been going on at the lake," Frank said.

"Well, you're out of luck. John and I are here every night but Tuesday and Wednesday," Vinnie said.

"And you're *in* luck," Frank said as he collected his food and his change. "That's pretty good proof you're not involved."

Vinnie looked at Frank in surprise. "I thought you were trying to pin this on us."

"No way. I'm trying to prove Ray is innocent," Frank said. "And if you guys are found innocent in the process, then all the better."

Before leaving the shop, Frank went to the pay phone and looked up the number for Tuttle's Bait Shop in the phone book. When he dialed the number, Ernie picked up the phone.

"Hi, Ernie, it's Frank Hardy. I was wondering if I could talk to Stu or Neil," Frank said. He wasn't at all surprised when Ernie told him they weren't home.

When Frank got back to the van, Joe was ready to eat. "I guess that game really got my appetite going," he said as he devoured his cheeseburger.

"Vinnie and John were working," Frank said between bites. "And for what it's worth, I called Tuttle's, and Stu and Neil weren't there."

"You think they're following us?" Joe asked.

"I was thinking we should maybe check around the hangouts in town and see if anyone has seen them," Frank said.

Frank pulled out of the lot and drove toward downtown Bayport. They weren't a dozen yards from Burger World when he saw the headlights in his mirror again.

"Joe, we've still got company," Frank said.

Joe looked at the passenger-side mirror. "Looks like the same lights to me."

As they drove through town, they saw a police cruiser parked near the Dew Drop Inn. Frank pulled next to the cruiser and saw that Con Riley was behind the wheel.

"Hey, Con, how's it going?" Frank called out.

"Tired. I'm working a double shift, Frank. How's your investigation going?" Con replied.

"Good. Listen, I have a question for you. Have you ever seen Ernie's grandsons hitchhiking into town at night or hanging out in any of the local joints?" Frank asked.

Riley thought for a moment. "No, can't say I have. And you know I stop in pretty much everywhere during my shift. Do you think they're in on something?"

"It would be nice to have some proof before we say anything," Frank said. "And, Con, do me a favor. I think someone's been following us. As we pull away, see if you notice anyone behind me."

Frank backed the van onto the road. There was no sign of a vehicle behind him.

"Do you think they took off when they saw Con's car?" Joe asked.

"Your guess is as good as mine," Frank said.

A half mile farther up the road, they came to an intersection where the road they were on came to an end. They would have to turn right or left.

"I can't see a thing," Frank said. With the trees and mounds of plowed snow, it was difficult to see much in either direction.

"No headlights, either," Joe said. He peered into the darkness but saw nothing coming. "I guess the coast is clear."

Preparing to turn right, Frank slowly pulled into the intersection, when suddenly they heard the distinct whir of tires on the snow. "Frank!" Joe screamed as a pickup truck came racing straight at them with its lights off.

10 Thin Ice!

Frank slammed on the gas, and the van shot across the road as the truck roared by just behind them. The van bounced over the curb and into a ditch on the far side of the road, coming to a stop at a steep angle. The front bumper pressed into the ditch, and the back wheels were spinning a foot in the air. Frank and Joe lurched forward but were held back by their seat belts.

"Are you all right?" Frank asked as he tried to sit up.

"I'm okay," Joe responded. "Did you get a look at it?"

"A pickup, dark blue, maybe green. I'm not sure," Frank said.

It took some effort to get out of the van because when they released their seat belts, they fell forward onto the dashboard.

84

"Sorry about driving into a ditch," Frank said as they climbed out of the van.

"Better than getting broadsided," Joe said.

Frank inspected the front of the van, which was pressed into the snow. "It doesn't look too bad," he said.

"We're not getting it back on the road without help," Joe said.

"I'll go call Hank," Frank said.

Joe looked down the dark streets. There were no cars to be seen.

"They're not following us now," Joe said.

"I'm pretty sure they were the ones who just ran us off the road," Frank said.

Frank walked back toward town and went to the pay phone by the all-night deli to call Hank. Then he went inside and bought two cups of hot chocolate so he and Joe could warm up.

When Hank arrived, he walked around the van and whistled loudly. "You guys sure are magnets for trouble," he said as he attached a cable to the rear of the van.

"Thanks for getting here so fast," Joe said.

"You've got to catch these guys before anyone else gets hurt," Hank said. He walked back to his truck to start hauling the van up. It didn't take him long to get the van back on the road. Frank and Joe were relieved to see there was no serious damage, just some scratches to the paint.

"Maybe you guys ought to take the rest of the night off," Hank said. "I'd say you deserve it."

"Sounds good to me," Frank agreed.

* * *

When they got home, their father, Fenton Hardy, was in his study. Frank and Joe filled him in on their investigation.

"So you suspect Tuttle and his grandsons?" Fenton asked.

"Yeah, but we can't figure out a motive for Ernie," Joe said.

"He may need the money," Fenton said.

"Why? He has all that land," Frank said.

"And he owes a lot of money on it," Fenton said. "He hasn't paid his real estate taxes for the last few years. He refuses to sell even an acre or two, which would be plenty to pay off what he owes."

"So maybe it is the three of them working together," Joe suggested.

"I think it's time we stop by his shop and pick up some bait," Frank said. "What're you doing after school tomorrow, Joe?"

"I was thinking of doing a little fishing," Joe replied.

"Excellent!" Frank cheered.

Frank and Joe drove out to Tuttle's the next day after school. As they pulled into the large dirt lot in front of the shop, Joe saw Ernie's truck—a dark blue pickup with rust patches around the wheels—parked by the door.

"Frank, do you think that was the truck that was following us last night?" Joe asked.

"I'd bet money on it," Frank said.

"Let's see if we can get everyone outside and then one of us can go in and search the place," Joe said.

"I'll tell them we want to take up ice fishing," Frank said.

Inside they found Ernie behind the counter, fussing with a display of floats.

"So, it's the Hardy boys," Ernie said.

"Hey, Ernie—how're you doing?" Joe asked.

"I was doing better before you got here," Ernie said.

"Are you mad at us for something?" Frank asked, not sure if Ernie was joking.

"I saw you playing hockey with those punks yesterday," Ernie snarled.

"Someone had to teach them a lesson," Joe said proudly. "We whipped them."

"I'd whip them good if I could," Ernie mumbled.

"It sure is packed in here," Frank said. He looked around the crowded shop. There were racks on the walls with everything one could need for fishing: rods, reels, tackle boxes, fishing line, floats, weights, pliers, and hooks. There were nets with long handles, carrying cans, and even a wooden sled box.

"Do you sell a lot of this gear?" Joe asked as he walked down an aisle lined with the latest high-tech fishing equipment, small outboard motors, and electronic fish finders with little computer screens that displayed the terrain at the bottom of the lake. There were handheld global positioning satellite systems that could give a location down to a few feet by figuring the distance from satellites.

"All that electronic junk is for amateurs," Ernie grumbled.

"Really?" Frank said. "I'd think only the pros would invest in this kind of equipment."

"Are you kidding?" Ernie scoffed. "A real fisherman doesn't need a satellite to tell him where the fish are."

"Why do you keep it in stock if you feel that way?" Frank asked.

"I didn't say I wouldn't take money from amateurs; I just said they were the only ones dumb enough to buy this junk." Ernie laughed.

Joe examined the sled box that was for sale. Though he didn't have a measuring tape, he was nearly certain it fit the marks they had seen at the Dixon place.

"What's this for?" Joe asked.

"You boys don't know anything, do you?" Ernie said.

"We're trying to learn," Frank said, the hint of a smile on his lips.

"It's a sled box, boys. You use it to put your gear in. Saves you from straining your back. You just slide it across the ice," Ernie explained. "You can also sit on it while you're fishing."

"Where'd you get it?" Frank asked.

"I make 'em myself," Ernie said. "I've sold eight of them this year already."

"Are they all the same?" Joe asked.

"I don't paint 'em designer colors, if that's what you're asking. They work, don't they?" Ernie said with a touch of pride.

"Ernie, did I see your truck in town last night?" Joe asked.

"Could be," Ernie said. "Stu and Neil had some errands."

"Are Stu and Neil around?" Frank asked.

"They're out fishing," Ernie said.

"They must know the good spots," Joe said.

"They're learning," Ernie said.

"Maybe you could show us some of those spots, Ernie?" Frank asked.

"Why? Are you town boys going to take up ice fishing?" Ernie asked in disbelief.

"We're thinking about it," Frank replied. "We've been spending so much time around here, we figure we ought to at least try."

"There's not much to it, if you can take the cold," Ernie said.

"Where should we start fishing?" Frank asked.

"There's a bunch of places," Ernie said, making no sign that he was going to come out from behind the counter.

"Would you mind pointing them out?" Frank asked, waving for Ernie to come outside.

"You're not going to leave me in peace until I do, are you?" Ernie said.

"No, sir," Frank said.

Ernie got up from his chair and followed Frank out the door.

There was an open door at the back of the store leading to the room where Ernie lived. The moment that Frank and Ernie left the shop, Joe ran to the back and slipped into Ernie's living quarters. It was just one large room cluttered with furniture. There was a kitchen at one end and a bathroom at the other. Ernie had a bed by a window, and Stu and Neil had sleeping bags on a pair of cots. Their duffel bags had clothes pouring out on the floor. It looked like the last day of a three-week camping trip during which no one had cleaned anything.

Joe didn't know how long Frank was going to keep Ernie outside. He scanned the objects on the small table between the two cots, but there was nothing except the usual suspects: some change and pencil stubs. He quickly looked through Ernie's dresser drawers, then went to the kitchen and checked the cabinets. If there was any stolen loot in the room, it must have been hidden in the walls or under the floorboards, he decided.

Next to the phone, Joe saw a notepad covered with telephone numbers. He took the photocopy of the note that came through their van window from his pocket and compared the handwriting to the various scribbles on the pad. None of it matched.

The note was written on a piece of paper nearly the same size as the notepad, the only difference being that one edge of the page was torn off. Joe saw that the bottom of the pad had the words Miller's Reels on it. Joe was sure the note was from the same pad but that someone had torn the Miller's Reels part off to make it a blank sheet. Joe tore off a blank piece from the pad.

After searching for a full five minutes, Joe hadn't come up with anything. He peeked out the window and saw that Frank and Ernie were still by the lake.

Joe looked over the room, thinking of where he would hide something. He lifted up the sleeping bags. Then he got down on the floor and looked

90

underneath the cots. He saw a small piece of paper folded up and wedged under the canvas of one of the cots.

It was a list of numbers written in two columns. Joe couldn't make much sense of it, but he was certain there was something to it. Why else would it be hidden? Joe grabbed a pencil and copied the numbers on the piece of paper he'd taken from the pad and then returned the original to its hiding place.

He slipped back into the shop just as Frank and Ernie came through the front door.

"So you want any fishing gear?" Ernie asked.

"Not ready yet. We're going to start out with Hank," Frank said as he looked over at Joe. Joe gave him a nod to let him know he'd found something.

"So why are you wasting my time asking for fishing spots?" Ernie snapped as he took his seat behind the counter.

"Because you're the one who knows the good ones," Joe said.

This answer seemed to satisfy Ernie, who picked up a magazine and began to leaf through it.

"By the way, we wanted to ask Stu and Neil if they'd seen anything since the fire you had. Do you know where they are?" Frank asked.

"Didn't you see them on the lake?" Ernie said as he waved to the window.

"No, but we'll go look now. Thanks for all your help," Frank said as he held the door open for Joe.

As the Hardys walked down the hill to the lake, Frank looked back to see if Ernie was watching them.

"What did you find?" Frank asked.

"Look at this," Joe said as he handed Frank the piece of paper. "I think the paper came from the same pad as the note we got airmailed to us at the Kwans'."

"What about the handwriting?" Frank asked.

"Not a match. Whoever wrote the note probably used his or her left hand or something so we wouldn't be able to trace it. But look at the paper. It's definitely the same. And there's a part that's torn off," Joe said, pointing.

"What do you think these numbers mean?" Frank asked.

"No idea," Joe replied.

"Is that Neil and Stu over there?" Frank said as he pointed to two men fishing.

"Hey, guys!" Joe called.

Neil and Stu waved to the Hardys. But as Frank and Joe came toward them, Neil and Stu began to walk farther down the lake—away from them.

"Don't they see we're trying to catch up to them?" Joe asked.

"Maybe that's why they're moving away," Frank said.

After a few more steps, Joe felt the ice beneath his foot give way slightly. He heard a squishing sound.

"Frank, stop," Joe warned.

Frank froze in his tracks. "What?"

"Thin ice," Joe said. "It's really dangerous where you are."

Frank carefully got down on all fours to spread

his weight more fully. "Get down slowly," he called to Joe, who was a few feet ahead of him.

Frank could see Joe begin to crouch down with his hands outstretched in front of him. There was a loud crack, followed by a splash, and then Joe was gone.

11 Chilled to the Bone

"Joe!" Frank expected to see Joe pop up through the hole in the ice. But after the splash, he heard nothing. Frank lay down on the ice and crawled over to look into the hole. He saw only chunks of ice floating in the frigid water.

Frank began to shout as he slid back away from the hole. "Help! My brother's fallen in!"

In an instant, ice fishermen came running. Some carried heavy steel ice bars, others held their augers. At first Frank was shocked to see that they weren't coming toward him but rather to various spots about a dozen yards away.

"Over here," one of the fishermen shouted to Frank. "The current's got him!"

The current! Even though the surface of the lake was frozen, the water underneath was still moving,

Frank realized. That was why Joe hadn't come back up through the hole.

Frank ran to help the fishermen, who were frantically attacking the ice, some with axes, others drilling with power augers. Frank tried to see Joe through the milky whiteness of the ice. He finally caught a glimpse of Joe's yellow coat moving beneath the surface.

"He's here; I'm right over him," Frank shouted to the fishermen.

Frank held out his arm in the direction Joe was drifting so the men could make holes in the ice along Joe's route.

Frank looked ahead to see if there were any holes where Joe was headed. Frank ran to the nearest hole, a nine-inch circle cut with a power auger. He lay on the ice and reached his arm into the cold water, hoping he'd be able to grab Joe as he drifted by. Fishermen circled Frank, their tools at the ready.

"Here he comes," one of the men called.

Frank saw the yellow of Joe's parka and reached deep into the hole to grab the sleeve. He pulled the sleeve so that Joe's head came to the hole. Joe's face popped into the hole, and he took a deep breath.

The fishermen sprang into action, attacking the ice around the hole to make it big enough to pull Joe through.

"Joe, are you okay?" Frank said as he held on to his brother.

"Cold . . ." Joe said.

"Stay with me. We'll get you out in a second," Frank said. But he knew they didn't have a lot of time to spare. Joe had already been in the water a minute or two. Frank could see he was having trouble breathing. He knew it was partly because his muscles were so tight from the cold.

As the fishermen expanded the hole, Frank tried to pull Joe out. One of the fishermen grabbed Joe's other sleeve and others took hold of Frank to make sure he didn't get pulled in himself. In a few moments, they had Joe out and lying on the ice.

"I'm really cold, Frank," Joe said through his chattering teeth.

"I know, we'll get you warm," Frank said.

"Quick, let's get him to Tuttle's," one of the fishermen said.

"No, take him to the Kwans'," Frank said. Not only did he distrust Ernie, he remembered that Mrs. Kwan was a nurse.

Erik Fernandez, one of the fishermen, drove his snowmobile, trailing one of Ernie's homemade sleds, up beside Joe on the ice. They rolled Joe onto the sled and Frank held his head as Fernandez took off for the Kwans' house.

"You still with me, Joe?" Frank asked as he looked at his brother's bluish lips.

Joe said something, but Frank couldn't hear him over the roar of the snowmobile. He leaned over until his ear was an inch from Joe's mouth.

"I can't feel my feet," Joe whispered. Frank knew this was a dangerous time. Even though Joe was out of the water, his clothes were soaked and starting to freeze in the cold air.

"Stay with me, Joe," Frank said. With only a few moments before they reached the Kwans', Frank looked around the lake and saw that there was no sign of Stu or Neil. He couldn't be sure they had drawn them onto the thin ice on purpose, but it sure seemed that way.

Frank looked ahead to the Kwans' house and saw Sarah waving at them. Erik drove the snowmobile right up to the Kwans' back door.

"Joe fell in," Frank said as he lifted his brother's nearly frozen body from the sled with Erik's help.

"We saw you pull him out," Sarah said. "My mom's getting ready for him."

Frank and Erik brought Joe into the house.

Mrs. Kwan was all business. "Take Joe up to the bathroom and get those clothes off him. Sarah, put some water on to boil. I'll be right up."

Erik and Frank carried Joe upstairs to the bathroom. Mrs. Kwan had filled the tub with hot water. Frank and Erik had Joe stripped to his underwear when Mrs. Kwan walked in.

"This is no time for modesty. Get those wet things off him," she ordered.

Frank and Erik did as they were told and then lowered Joe into the warm water. Joe let out a shudder as the heat enveloped him.

"Keep an eye on him. I'll bring something hot for him to drink. The ambulance should be here in a minute," Mrs. Kwan said.

"Is he going to be all right?" Frank asked Mrs. Kwan.

"He wasn't in for long, was he?" she asked.

"I don't know, maybe three minutes at most,"

97

Frank said. "He was conscious when we got him out."

"He should be fine," Mrs. Kwan said with the knowing confidence of a professional.

Joe slowly began to seem more awake, and his color was improving.

Mrs. Kwan brought up a mug of hot water for Joe to drink. "It'll warm him up from the inside," she said.

By the time the paramedics arrived, Joe was sitting up in the tub, looking almost normal.

One of the paramedics came into the bathroom and asked Frank, "How's he doing?"

"I'm okay," Joe said.

The paramedic checked Joe's temperature and then took his pulse and blood pressure. "You're lucky they got you out so fast," he said.

"I'd be luckier if I hadn't fallen in to begin with," Joe said.

"Is he going to be all right?" Frank asked the paramedic.

"To be on the safe side, we could take him to the hospital for more tests. But honestly, there isn't much they can do for him that you can't do here. Keep him warm and take his temperature periodically to make sure he's okay," he said.

Frank turned to Mrs. Kwan, who was standing in the doorway. "What do you think Mrs. Kwan? Should we go to the hospital?"

"If his vital signs are all right, I think he'll be fine," she said.

"Then I'll stay. The food's much better here than at the hospital," Joe said.

The paramedics left, and Mrs. Kwan got Joe a robe and heavy socks so he'd have something to wear while she put his clothes into the dryer.

"Go have a seat by the fire," she suggested.

Joe put on the robe, but he had an embarrassed look on his face.

"What's the matter?" Frank asked.

"I feel weird hanging around here in a bathrobe," Joe said. "I mean, there's a girl from school here."

"It's either that or—nothing," Frank said.

Joe thought for a moment. "Bathrobe," he announced.

Frank watched Joe go down the stairs, being sure his brother was really as strong as he claimed after his ordeal. Soon they were sitting by the fire, drinking hot chocolate.

"What do you think happened out there?" Joe asked Frank as he felt the warmth of the fire on his feet.

"You mean with Neil and Stu?" Frank asked.

"Yeah," Joe said.

"It looks like they drew us onto the thin ice on purpose," Frank said.

"That's what I thought," Joe said, anger rising in his voice. "Then what did they do?"

"You'll be comforted to know that my first response was to go after you," Frank said. "I didn't give them a second thought."

"For which I'm grateful," Joe said.

"But when I did look up, I didn't see them anywhere," Frank recalled.

99

"They didn't come to my rescue?" Joe said, a hint of bitterness in his voice.

"Nope."

Just then Sarah walked into the room. "Joe, this is the stuff that was in your pockets," she said. "I should get you a plastic bag for it."

"That'd be great," Joe said as he took the things from Sarah. He laid his wallet in front of the fire. "Maybe it'll dry here."

Joe took out his driver's license, his money, and a picture of him and Frank at the beach with Callie and Iola.

"Oh, and there was this," Sarah said. She handed him the sheet of paper with the numbers he had copied down at Tuttle's.

"I forgot about that," Joe said as he carefully unfolded the soggy paper. The ink had bled into the paper, but the numbers were still readable.

Frank came over and took a look. "Do you think they read in descending order as columns or across as pairs?" Frank asked.

"Beats me," Joe said.

They looked at the numbers for some time, but the pattern eluded them.

"You know who could probably figure this out?" Joe said. "Phil."

"Good idea," Frank said. "We need to see him about the heat in the van, anyway."

The phone rang, and Mrs. Kwan went to answer it. "It's for either one of you boys," she called from the kitchen extension.

"Sit tight, Joe," Frank said. "I'll get it."

Mrs. Kwan handed Frank the receiver but stayed right where she was, next to Frank.

"Frank Hardy, here," he said clearly into the phone.

Mrs. Kwan watched Frank's face get darker and darker. She followed every syllable of Frank's side of the conversation.

"Uh-huh . . . okay . . . uh-huh, yep. Gotcha. May I ask who's calling?" After a pause, Frank turned around and hung the receiver back on the wall mount.

"What was that all about?" asked Mrs. Kwan.

"Let's go back by the fire so I have to say this only once," Frank recommended.

"Who was that, bro?" asked Joe.

"I don't know," Frank answered. "But it was a man, and he wanted me to relay a message to the Kwans.

Mrs. Kwan's face turned slightly pale. "What is it?"

"The caller wants you to know that you and your family are in big trouble—"

"What?" Sarah cried.

"Shh," said her mother. "What else?"

"Seems you're in danger for helping out the Hardy boys."

At that instant, a loud crack echoed from nearby. It was the unmistakable sound of a gunshot.

12 Coming Through!

"Down, everyone, now!" Frank commanded. He grabbed hold of Mrs. Kwan and Sarah and threw them, along with himself, to the floor. They waited, but there was nothing more to be heard.

"Stay down," Frank whispered. "They may simply be waiting for us to show ourselves." Frank pushed himself up to his hands, then crouched for a split second before sprinting to the front door, where he stopped.

"Frank!" Joe cried in a hoarse whisper. "What are you doing? You're going to get yourself killed! And Mom will never forgive me."

"Someone's got to check this out," Frank replied. "Do you want to?"

"No, no, Frank," Joe said, shaking his head. "It's your turn to be the hero."

"Thanks, bro." With that, Frank threw open the

door and flew out in a spiral, landing in the bushes against the house for cover.

There was silence. Joe strained his ears but could hear only an occasional scraping as Frank made a circuit of the house on his hands and knees. It seemed forever that they sat or lay on the floor waiting.

Finally, there was another noise. It was a knock on the front door.

"Don't answer it!" Sarah shrieked.

"It's okay." A muffled voice, but definitely Frank's muffled voice, came through the door.

Sarah herself went to the door. She peeked out the peephole and saw Frank Hardy holding a large branch.

"Well, you can be glad it was just a branch they broke to make that noise instead of real gunfire," Frank said as he stood the tree branch in the corner.

"But that's from Hiromi's Japanese feathered maple," Mrs. Kwan complained. "He'll be furious."

Frank and Joe exchanged looks and decided wordlessly that it was time to be going.

Once Joe was dressed, he and Frank left to go see Phil.

"We have to wrap this up soon," Frank said as they drove down the narrow road through the woods. "I don't want the Kwans all upset about that phone call."

"So other than the fact that every circumstance points to the Tuttles, what do we have?" Frank asked.

"Not much," Joe said. "Make that nothing."

"Maybe we should ask Con Riley to check if any of the stolen stuff has turned up in Maryland, where Stu and Neil are from," Frank said.

"Already done, bro," Joe said. "I called him between classes. He's working that angle."

They found Phil in his basement at a large workbench. He had computer parts strewn all around him while he concentrated on a tiny circuit board.

"Hey, Phil. What's up?" Joe said.

Phil took off his safety goggles and looked to see who had come in.

"Frank and Joe, I've been thinking about you," he said. "I think I've figured out how to heat that van of yours."

"First, we have something we want you to look at," Joe said. He reached into his pocket for the page of numbers and handed it to Phil.

"Looks like it's been through the wash," Phil said as he took the paper, which was now stiff and weather-beaten.

"I went swimming in the lake," Joe said.

"Are you crazy?" Phil asked.

"I didn't exactly plan it," Joe said.

"This list may have something to do with the robberies at the lake," Frank said.

"Chet told me some house sitter got beaten up pretty bad," Phil said. He looked at the list of numbers.

"Let's go upstairs," Phil said as he led them to his room.

"Hey, can I use your phone?" Joe asked.

"Sure. You know where it is." Phil waved him in the direction of the kitchen.

"I'm going to see if Con has gotten anything," Joe told his brother, and took off.

"Just remember, the phone is the little white box on the counter, not the big white box on the floor that is cold and has food in it," his brother called after him.

Frank couldn't believe all the electronic gadgets Phil had stacked against every inch of wall space. There were wires running everywhere.

Phil sat down at his computer and began typing in the numbers from Joe's list.

"Let's see if there's any pattern to these two columns," Phil said.

Frank watched Phil enter the numbers into the computer. He then ran a number of mathematical tests against them.

"What have you got?" Frank asked.

"Nothing so far," Phil said.

"Is it some kind of code?" Frank asked.

"I doubt it," Phil said. "You see all the numbers in the first column start with seventy-three and those in the second column start with forty. Then we have periods and another pair and another pair . . ."

Frank looked over Phil's shoulder at the numbers on the screen.

"I can't believe I've been such an idiot," Frank said. "Phil, do you have an atlas?"

"Sure, why?" Phil said as he got an atlas off a bookshelf.

"Longitude and latitude," Frank said.

Phil let out a big smile. "Of course. But we don't need an atlas."

Phil pulled a map program up onto the screen. He used the mouse to create a box around the area defined by longitude 73 and latitude 40. He then enlarged the box.

"New York," Frank said.

Phil typed in the coordinates from the list. Then he hit the return button and the computer zoomed in closer on the map.

"Bayport," Phil said as a map of their town filled the screen. "Let's go closer."

Phil typed in the last digits of the first set of coordinates. He hit the enter key and the map zoomed in closer. A red X began flashing right in Pineview Lake.

"That's your spot," Phil said proudly.

"In the lake?" Frank asked.

"Yup," Phil said.

Joe came into the room. "I talked to Riley. He hasn't gotten anything positive yet, but he said he's still got a few places to call."

"Great. Joe, take a look," Frank said.

"The numbers on your list were latitude and longitude," Phil explained.

"Do the next one," Frank said.

Phil repeated the procedure and again the computer flashed a red X in Pineview Lake.

"Good fishing spots?" Frank suggested half-heartedly.

"Why hide a list of good fishing spots under your mattress?" Joe asked.

"To keep them secret?" Frank said.

"Ernie hates this high-tech stuff," Joe reminded him. "He probably wouldn't know what this list was if he did see it."

Phil continued punching the numbers into the program, producing more red X's on the lake.

"I think we ought to get to the lake and check these out," Frank said. "Phil, can you print a map with those locations?"

"I can do better than that," Phil said. He went to a shelf full of small electronic devices and pulled out something that looked like a cellular phone with a large LCD screen. "We'll use this. Global positioning satellite system," Phil explained. "It can tell you exactly where you are, using satellites to triangulate your position. We'll hit these spots within a few feet. When do we go?"

"Now, if everyone's up for it," Frank said as he looked over at Joe.

"I'm used to the cold," Joe said with a smile.

They piled into the van, Phil carrying the GPS unit and the map with the X's.

By the time they reached the lake, it was dark and the night was bleak. Snow was falling. Clouds blocked the moonlight and the cold wind tore through their layers of clothing.

"You guys really know how to have a good time," Phil said as he bundled his coat tighter.

"We don't exactly pick our spots," Joe said.

"Let's not take any chances," Frank said. He stripped some branches for walking sticks.

"I've learned my lesson, thank you very much," Joe said as he helped with the branches.

Soon they were out on the lake, tapping their way

toward the nearest one of the spots on Phil's map. While Phil concentrated on the map and the green-ish glow of the GPS screen, Frank tapped along in front of them. Joe brought up the rear, using his flashlight to make sure they were alone on the lake.

"Can you guys see anything?" Phil asked.

"Yeah, snow," Frank said.

"We're here," Phil shouted over the roar of a gust of wind. "So what are we looking for?"

"I wish I could tell you," Frank said.

"Do you think maybe it's a guide for which houses to rob?" Phil said as he tried to see the houses through the falling snow.

"Beats me. Let's see if anyone's been fishing here," Joe suggested.

This was easier said than done because fresh snow covered the ice. Joe used his foot to push the snow away from the point where Phil had stopped. Frank and Phil did the same. After a few minutes, they had cleared the snow in a circle about eight feet across. Joe scanned the ice with his flashlight.

"See anything?" Phil asked.

The storm kept fresh snow streaking across the spot they had cleared.

"This is crazy," Phil said as the biting wind whipped his face.

"Welcome to detective work," Joe said.

"I prefer working with you guys indoors," Phil said.

Frank got down on his hands and knees.

"Thin ice?" Joe asked with concern in his voice as he saw his brother drop to the ice.

"No, I felt something," Frank said.

Joe shone his flashlight where Frank pointed. Frank could see an indentation in the ice, a little smaller than a manhole cover.

"There was a hole here, all right," Frank said. "See the ridge? It's frozen back over."

Joe trained his flashlight on the spot. The beams caught something, a shiny object frozen into the ice at one edge of the ridge.

"What's that?" Joe asked.

Frank crawled to the spot and brushed away the stray flakes that were gathering. "Looks like a piece of tinfoil."

"Can you believe people litter like that?" Phil said with disgust.

"Pretty stupid," Frank agreed.

"So what do you say, should we move on to the next spot?" Joe asked.

"I'm going to freeze if we don't get moving," Phil said.

"Okay, let's roll," Frank said as he got up from the ice.

They found the next spot and looked around the ice as they had in the place before. They found what they thought was another hole that had frozen over, but it was difficult to be certain. The ice was mottled with refrozen patches where snow had been stuck between layers of lake ice.

"Can't see much of anything here," Frank said, frustrated that they hadn't found a definite pattern. "Let's check another."

"It's cold out here," Phil protested.

"Yes, it is," Frank said as he took a look at Phil's map.

At the third spot, they repeated their steps, clearing a circle and examining the ice. This spot was much like the first one. They found some ridges at the edge of what had likely been a refrozen hole. In the middle of this one was another wad of tinfoil.

"Look—" Phil began.

"Shh!" Joe said as he turned off his flashlight. Frank and Phil turned off their flashlights, too.

"What is it?" Phil whispered.

"I heard something," Joe whispered. "Like an engine."

The ice beneath them rumbled. The rumbling grew stronger and then Joe heard the unmistakable sound of an engine roaring to life. He quickly turned on his flashlight and waved it in the direction of the noise. The light caught the gleam of shining chrome.

"Run!" Frank shouted.

Frank and Phil dove to one side and Joe ran to the other just as a truck came barreling right at them. It missed Frank by inches. Just as it went by, he saw the words painted on the door: Green's Salvage.

13 Something's Fishy

The truck roared by and disappeared into the darkness.

"Joe, you okay?" Frank called out.

"Yeah. You guys?" Joe replied.

"I'm okay," Phil said, "but I've had enough."

"We must be onto something," Joe said as he looked around in the darkness for the truck.

"That was Hank's truck," Frank said, getting to his feet.

"We'd better make sure he's okay," Joe said. He searched for his walking stick. He wasn't going to risk falling through the ice on the way back to the van.

"Do you think they were really trying to kill us?" Phil asked.

"I doubt it," Frank said. "They came through only once."

"They were just trying to scare us. Hurting us would have been a bonus," Joe added.

Soon they were back in the van and on the road that led to Green's Salvage. When they got there, Frank pulled the van off the road opposite the driveway.

"Look at that," Frank said, pointing at the entrance to Green's. "Fresh tire tracks."

They got out of the van, and Frank went to inspect the tracks.

"Not much snow. They must have been here within the last hour or so," Frank said.

"You notice something missing?" Joe asked.

Frank looked around and listened to the howling wind as it made eerie whistling sounds through the junked cars.

"Where's Red?" Frank asked.

Hank's dog wasn't barking.

"Red? Here, boy," Joe called out.

Frank took the flashlight from Joe, went to the office, and shined the flashlight in the window. He saw the furniture and newspapers strewn about. Then he saw a slab of raw meat on the floor. Next to the meat was Red.

Frank continued looking. "There's something."

Joe and Phil peered in and saw Red.

"He's just sleeping, right?" Phil asked.

Frank saw the dog's ribs moving. "He's breathing. My guess is he's been drugged."

"Where's Hank?" Joe asked.

"We'd better look around," Frank said. "Let's split up."

They each walked down a different row of

broken-down cars, scanning the ground, looking for footprints in the snow. But there were so many prints it was difficult to tell which were fresh.

Many of the cars were crushed, stacked three and four high. Others had been burned down to the metal and were missing doors and bumpers and fender panels.

"I heard something," Joe called out.

Frank and Phil came running.

"Did you hear that banging?" Joe asked.

"Where did it come from?" Phil asked.

They listened for a sound in the windy night. Then they all heard the banging.

"Hank? Hank, is that you?" Joe called out.

There were two loud knocks from a pile-up of old sedans. The windows were gone, along with some doors, Joe noticed. But all of the cars had their trunks intact, though dented.

"Over here," Joe said as he ran to the cars.

The banging seemed to be coming from the trunk of the bottom car. Joe knocked back, but even that rather small shock sent the hulking remains of the big sedan on top of the pile rocking.

Frank shined his flashlight on the sedan perched precariously on top. "Take it easy, Joe. That one on top's going to fall," he said.

"Get me out!" Hank's muffled voice came from inside the trunk of the car on the bottom.

"We'll have you out in a minute, Hank," Joe called to him.

"Phil, go find a crowbar," Frank said. "I think if we climb up, we can push that top one off."

"If we step on the bottom one, that might shift the balance," Joe suggested.

Frank examined the stack. "You're right."

"We just have to go for it," Joe said as Phil returned with a crowbar.

Joe leaned over the trunk in which Hank was locked. "Hank, we've got a problem. The car on top looks like it might come down."

"Maybe we can use the crane to get that top car off," Phil suggested.

"No!" Hank shouted from inside the trunk. "The crane doesn't work. I was going to fix it."

"Well, then, here goes," Joe said as he carefully wedged the crowbar into the space below the lid of the trunk. "Okay, Hank. Be ready to jump out of there," Joe said as he began to pry open the trunk.

The metal made a sharp creaking sound, and the car dipped from the force of Joe's pressure.

Frank kept his flashlight trained on the car on top. The back end began to dip lower. "Joe, easy," he called to his brother.

Joe eased up on the crowbar. "I'm going to have to use some force."

"I know, just take it slow," Frank said as the car on top steadied. "Okay, try again."

Joe shoved the crowbar a few inches farther into the trunk and lifted, using a slow, steady motion and the power of his muscular legs. The lid of the trunk began to bend.

"Easy," Frank called to him.

Joe kept the force steady, waiting for the top car to stop rocking.

"Okay, Hank, here we go," Joe said.

He gave the crowbar another pull. The trunk door popped open. The second car lurched, and the one on top began to swing.

Hank was struggling to sit up. He was moving too slowly. Joe dropped the crowbar and grabbed Hank's arm.

"Look out!" Phil shouted.

The top car was sliding backward. Phil ran to the side while Frank jumped to help Hank. Frank and Joe got Hank out of the trunk, and they all fell onto the snow just to the side of the stack of cars. The big sedan slid down the back of the pile of cars and crashed, sending clouds of snow and dirt up over the Hardys and Hank.

The top car was now standing on its end, its hood crunched into the frozen ground.

"Let's get inside," Joe said.

"What made you guys come here?" Hank said. He was shivering and walking with a limp, numb from the cold.

"Someone came at us in your truck," Joe said. "In the middle of the lake."

As they approached the office, Hank began looking around frantically. "Where's Red?"

"He's inside. I think he's been drugged," Frank said.

Hank ran into the office, with the others following along. When the boys got inside, Hank was already on his knees, scooping Red into his arms.

"What did they do to you, boy?" Hank said.

Frank went over to the half-eaten piece of meat.

He saw that there was white powder on the meat. "He'll be out for a while, Hank. It looks like someone sprinkled sleeping powder on this meat," Frank said.

"I hope he's okay," Hank said as he carried Red to the couch.

"I'll call the police," Joe said.

"Why don't you heat up some cider for Hank," Frank called to Joe.

"Coffee," Hank called out. "Black. Boiling. Thanks."

"Hank, who did this?" Frank asked.

"Two guys. I saw them just for a second. They put a bag over my head and carried me out."

"They say anything?" Frank asked.

"Just warned me," Hank said.

"Did you recognize the voices?" Frank asked.

"They were kind of familiar, but I couldn't place them," Hank said.

"Hank, any chance it was Ernie's grandsons?" Frank asked.

Hank stopped petting Red for a moment. "Are you kidding?"

"No, but I don't have any proof yet," Frank said.

"Honestly, I don't want to believe that, but yeah, it could have been them. They're about the right size. The guys were wearing black ski masks," Hank said.

Joe and Phil returned with a cup of steaming coffee for Hank.

"The police are on their way," Joe said.

"Hank, can I ask you some questions about the lake?" Frank said as he got the map of the locations on the lake and showed it to Hank. "Do these spots mean anything to you?"

"What do you mean?" Hank asked as he examined the map.

"Are they good for ice fishing?" Frank asked.

"You want to talk about fishing spots?" Hank asked in disbelief.

"Ernie's grandsons had this list of locations hidden," Frank said.

"You think it has something to do with all this?" Hank asked.

"We're trying to find out," Joe said.

"All right, then, let's take a look," Hank said. "Let me get my fishing journal." He went to his desk and pulled out a tattered map of the lake from it. The map was covered with his scribbled notes.

"Well, let's see . . . no, no." Hank looked at both maps side by side for a few minutes, shaking his head. "Are you sure this is for ice fishing?"

"No, we're not," Frank admitted.

"Because I sure haven't had much luck in these spots. Some of them are downright treacherous. You see this one here?" Hank said as he pointed to one of the red marks on Phil's map. "There's a pretty strong current under there—makes the ice unstable. And this one gets a lot of sun late in the day."

"So?" Joe asked.

"The sun melts the top of the ice and then it freezes again at night. That's weak ice. Not worth risking your life for a fish," Hank said.

"So whoever's using these locations has them pretty much to himself," Frank said.

117

"I'll say. But no one with any brains would use them. Maybe in a cold snap, with light equipment, you might be okay," Hank said.

As they were folding the maps, the police arrived. The officers took Hank's statement, along with the drugged slab of meat. They also took statements from Frank, Joe, and Phil about what they had seen out at the lake.

"Well, if that's it, I'd really like to get home," Phil said.

"Sure, we'll drop you off," Frank said as they got into the van.

"You know I'm available to help," Phil said.

"I thought you hated the cold," Joe said.

"I told you I can fix the heat in here," Phil said.

"I meant the cold on the lake," Joe said, and they all laughed.

Frank drove carefully through the snow-swept streets of town and dropped Phil off before heading home. Frank and Joe went over their clues.

"It's got to be Neil and Stu. Who else could have gotten into the junkyard on foot?" Joe said. "There was only one set of tire tracks at Hank's."

"Who else could have seen us on the lake in that snow?" Frank added. "I wouldn't mind getting another look inside Tuttle's shanty. We just need to think of a plan."

When they got home, it was late and everyone was in bed. Their folks had left the porch light on for them. As Frank and Joe came up the front steps, they saw something rolled in a piece of newspaper by the door.

"What do you think that is?" Joe asked.

Frank got closer. "It stinks."

"This whole thing stinks," Joe agreed.

"No, really—smell it," Frank said.

Joe leaned over and caught the unmistakable stench of dead fish. "Yuck."

Frank kicked the newspaper. As it rolled down the steps, it unraveled and made a jingling sound. A large fish fell out. There was a set of keys dangling from its mouth.

"Keys?" Joe said.

Frank took the keys out of the fish's mouth. He read the faded lettering on the key ring: "Green's Salvage."

"I think Hank's truck took a dive," Frank said. "It's swimming with the fishes now!"

14 Runaway!

"Let's call the police and tell them about the keys," Frank said as they went into the house.

"You think Hank's truck is at the bottom of the lake?" Joe asked.

"That's my guess," Frank said.

The police took the information and sent an officer over to the Hardys' to pick up the keys and the fish.

"We'd better call Hank," Frank said.

"Like his day wasn't bad enough already," Joe said.

But much to their surprise, Hank took the news fairly well.

"I'm okay and Red's okay. I can always get another truck," he said when he heard his truck was at the bottom of the lake.

The next day at school, Frank and Joe ran into Sarah and Phil between classes.

"How are things with your folks?" Frank asked Sarah.

"My dad's still freaking out about all the stuff going on by the lake. Are you guys getting anywhere finding out who's been doing all this?" she asked.

"Yeah, we're getting somewhere," Joe said.

"Can I tell my dad who it is?" Sarah asked, her face bright with excitement.

"We can't say anything yet," Frank said.

"I've been thinking about the other night," Phil said. "Maybe we didn't find anything because that snowstorm messed up the GPS readings."

Sarah looked at Phil as if he were speaking another language. "Well, good luck," she said, before running off to class.

"I feel lousy about her family's getting threatened," Frank said as he, Joe, and Phil went to class.

"We'll wrap this up in the next few days for sure," Joe said.

"We'd better," Frank said. "Hey, I've got an idea about how we can get into Ernie's shanty. We'll go to replace the door to Rizzo's cabin. That'll give us an excuse to do some snooping."

After school they picked up a piece of plywood and then stopped at Hank's.

"Have you recovered from last night?" Joe asked him.

"I was old and stiff before they locked me in that

121

trunk, and I'm still old and stiff now that I'm out," Hank said with a chuckle.

"Any word on your truck?" Frank asked.

"Not yet. The police are checking the lake," Hank said. "So, is there anything I can do to help out?"

"Actually, there is," Frank said. "We're going to do some looking around, and we need you to distract whoever is in Ernie's shop. Maybe you could talk fishing with Ernie for a while."

"Sure. Whatever you need," Hank said.

"Would you mind if Ray Nelson went with you?" Joe asked.

"Ray Nelson? Don't you think that's going to look kind of strange?" Hank said.

"Who else would he learn ice fishing from? His dad won't set foot in the area, and Ernie won't give him the time of day," Frank said.

"Ray's not such a bad guy and we may need some help out there today," Joe added.

"Well, all right, if it'll help put an end to all this," Hank said.

"Great. We'll give Ray a call and have him meet you here," Joe said.

With their backup forces arranged, Frank and Joe went to the lake.

Frank parked the van in the dirt lot next to Tuttle's Bait Shop. He saw Stu and Neil looking at them from the shop window as he and Joe walked down the sloping embankment to the lake. Their first stop was Ernie's shanty.

"Ernie? You in there?" Joe called out. "It's Frank and Joe Hardy."

"What do you want?" Ernie said.

Frank opened the door and saw Ernie hunched over one of the tiny trapdoors in the floor, watching his fishing line intently.

"Close the door, will you?" Ernie barked.

Joe followed his brother into the cramped space and closed the door behind him.

"Is this a social call?" Ernie said.

Frank and Joe looked around at the piles of junk. There were benches built into either side of the cabin. Joe noticed that the seats were hinged and had storage space underneath—making a good hiding place, he thought.

"We came to fix the door of Rizzo's shanty," Frank said.

"What's that got to do with me?" Ernie said without looking up from his fishing line.

"We wanted to ask you a favor," Joe began.

"Two favors, really," Frank added.

"You'd better ask quickly before you make it three," Ernie said.

"The truth is we don't know much about these ice shanties," Frank said.

"Look around, boys. There isn't much to them," Ernie said.

But Frank knew that Ernie wouldn't pass up the chance to give some orders.

"The thing is, we really want to do it right and avoid any trouble with Mr. Rizzo. If you wouldn't mind, we'd really appreciate it if you'd come over and just talk us through it," Frank said.

Ernie took the bait. "I could teach you boys a thing or two. What's the second favor?"

"We were hoping you'd let us plug in our tools at the shop," Joe said.

"Sure. Stu and Neil can help you," Ernie said as he reeled in his line. "The fish aren't biting anyway. Help me up," Ernie commanded.

Frank helped Ernie to his feet, and he and Joe followed him out across the ice to Rizzo's shanty.

"What did you do in there, anyway?" Ernie asked when they reached Rizzo's.

"Someone locked us in," Frank said, hoping to get some reaction from Ernie.

"You boys shouldn't be playing around in other people's stuff," Ernie said, giving no hint that he knew anything about the incident.

"We tried to patch it, but as you said the other day, maybe it's better to replace the whole door," Frank said.

"I'm going to take a look around and see what other people do about the hinges," Joe said as he walked away.

Ernie inspected the door to Rizzo's shanty. "I never cared for what Rizzo did here with the door frame. If it was me, I'd make the door bigger," he said.

"We weren't planning to change anything but the door," Frank said as he watched Joe over Ernie's shoulder.

Seeing that Frank was well on his way to learning how to build a shanty from scratch, Joe walked back to Ernie's shanty. He looked up the hill and saw that Hank and Ray were ready. Joe waved to them, and they entered the bait shop to distract Stu and Neil.

124

Joe slipped into Ernie's shanty. He quickly went to one of the benches and lifted the hinged seat. There was a tarp inside. Joe lifted the tarp, expecting to find stolen loot. He was disappointed to find only buckets filled with tools, a torn net, some hooks, and something that looked as if it might have been half a sandwich from the year before. But there was nothing the least bit suspicious.

Joe opened the second bench. Inside was a steel ice bar, a long gaff hook, some broken fishing rods, and spare reels. There was even a metal detector, the kind people used to find coins and things on the beach. But there was no sign of stolen loot.

Joe looked through one of the shanty windows and saw that Frank was still getting an earful from Ernie. He then checked out the other cubbyholes and shelves around the shanty but found nothing. He went to the door, made sure that no one was watching, and went outside.

Before rejoining Frank and Ernie, he walked around Ernie's shanty. In back, there was an odd-looking thing, like a huge suitcase, with two plastic halves. Heavy canvas poked out where the two pieces came together. It was a portable ice shelter. When opened, the two plastic halves formed the floor and the canvas hung over a collapsible frame. Joe saw that one of the two plastic sections was hinged so that the floor could open up for fishing.

Joe wandered back over to Rizzo's cabin, where Ernie was still explaining the art of shanty construction to Frank.

"Now, I think you can build it flush instead

of just slapping it on the outside," Ernie explained.

With Joe back, Frank could get on with the work at hand.

"All right, I think I see what we've got to do here," Frank said, hoping to bring Ernie's lecture to an end.

"Maybe I'll just stick around and make sure you boys don't mess it up," Ernie said.

"Let me get these measurements and we can go cut the wood," Frank said as he pulled a tape measure from his pocket.

While Frank and Joe were measuring the door, Hank and Ray came by with their fishing gear.

"Hey, there, Hank. I heard your truck went swimming," Ernie said as they walked by.

"Where'd you hear that?" Hank asked.

Frank and Joe were also curious, since they had told only Hank and the police about the incident on the lake and the keys in the fish.

"The police told me when they found it a little while ago," Ernie said. "Now, why on earth would you be driving on the ice down by Brown's Brook?"

"I wasn't. Someone stole it," Hank said.

"Well, that's what happens when you hang around with hoodlums," Ernie said as he looked at Ray.

Joe could see that Ray wasn't about to take that comment without a reaction. He ran over and took Ray by the arm.

"Hey, Ray, good luck fishing," Joe said.

"You'd better nail him," Ray grumbled to Joe.

"We can't if you blow it," Joe said, "so keep your cool."

Ray nodded and kept walking without causing an incident.

Frank and Joe went back up the hill to get the sheet of plywood out of the van. They placed it on a pair of sawhorses that Ernie kept for repairing the canoes he rented in the summer.

"What are you guys doing?" Neil called out from the shop.

"We need to fix the door on Rizzo's shanty," Frank said. If hearing this had any effect on Neil, he didn't let it show.

"We're going to need to plug in our saw," Joe called over to him.

"No problem," Neil said pleasantly.

"Those guys are something," Joe said quietly to Frank. "Pretty cool, considering they nearly killed us last night."

"They're slimy, no doubt about it," Frank said.

After Frank and Joe cut the wood to size, they each took an end of the door and walked back down the hill to the lake. With the door between them, it was difficult to walk very quickly. Frank slipped on the icy snow and fell to his knees. Joe grabbed the door.

Frank looked up the hill as he tried to get back on his feet. "Oh, no, not again!" he cried. "Get out of the way!" he shouted to Joe.

But Frank didn't think Joe was moving fast

127

enough. He shoved the door they were carrying between them as hard as he could toward Joe, which sent them both sprawling to the ground. Unfortunately, they hadn't cleared the runway. They both looked up to see their own van rolling and sliding down the slope. Its aim was perfect: two Hardys for the price of one.

15 Friend or Foe?

"Look out!" Joe yelled to the fishermen. Joe could still yell because he hadn't been hit by the runaway van after all. Just a few seconds before reaching Frank and Joe, the van had hit a patch of sheer ice. Its wheels had spun helplessly as it skidded wide of its mark and onto the frozen lake.

Frank saw the horrified looks of the few people on the lake as the van rolled right down the open lane between the rows of shanties. It finally came to a stop out on the ice.

Frank got up and brushed the snow off his clothes. "How'd that happen?"

"Someone must have released the parking brake, and I think I know who," Joe said. He began climbing up the hill to go after Stu and Neil.

"Calm down," Frank said, grabbing Joe's arm.

"Getting into a fight isn't going to prove anything. Let's get the van, finish Rizzo's door, and get some evidence."

Joe knew Frank was right, but the knowledge did little to calm his anger.

When they walked out onto the lake, some of the fishermen came out to scold them. "You boys have to be more careful. You could've killed someone."

Hearing this only made Joe angrier. Frank wasn't happy about it either, but he knew that objecting might make the situation worse.

"I'll drive," Joe insisted.

"Fine, but first roll down the windows and open the doors," Frank said. "Then if the van breaks through the ice, the doors may catch solid ice long enough for you to jump out."

"And the open windows are so I can swim out?" Joe asked.

"You seemed to enjoy the cold water so much last time," Frank said with a smile.

Joe started the van and drove slowly across the lake. The ice made some deep groaning sounds, but soon the van was on dry land. Joe didn't think they should leave the van at Ernie's, so they parked it in the Kwans' driveway, where they hoped no one would touch it.

They walked across the lake to get the wood they had left on the hillside, then went to fix Rizzo's shanty door. When they were done, they walked down to where Ray and Hank were fishing.

"How'd it go?" Ray asked.

"We didn't find anything incriminating," Joe said with disappointment in his voice.

"So, you catch anything?" Frank asked Ray.

"No offense, but I think this is about the most boring thing I've ever done," Ray said. He was sitting on an upturned bucket and had a short fishing pole in his hands.

"Well, look at what you're doing," Hank said. "The hole is freezing over with your line in it. You've got to keep it clear."

Hank handed Ray a large skimmer so he could scoop the newly forming ice out of the hole.

"Hank," Joe said, "what do you use a metal detector for?"

"To find metal," Hank said.

"No, I mean when you're ice fishing," Joe said.

"What are you talking about?" Hank asked.

"There was a metal detector in Ernie's shanty."

Hank was surprised. "A metal detector?"

"You know, like people use at the beach, with the long handle," Joe said.

"I've never heard of anyone using one for ice fishing," Hank said, trying to figure out how it could help find fish.

"And there was a collapsible shanty with a hinged floor," Joe said.

"You mean the trapdoor for fishing," Hank corrected him.

"No, the whole floor could be opened up," Joe insisted.

Hank looked perplexed.

"Is that weird?" Frank asked.

"Sure is," Hank said. "It would make the shanty too cold and you'd run the risk of the thing freezing into the ice."

"I think I'm getting it," Frank said as he began to see how all the pieces fit.

"You've got something?" Joe asked.

"Maybe. When we checked out those locations, what did we see?" Frank asked.

"Nothing," Joe said.

"No, we saw tinfoil," Frank said.

Joe began to see where Frank was headed.

"With the coordinates from your list and a metal detector, you could pinpoint those tinfoil balls exactly," Frank said.

"And with a big trapdoor, you could cut larger holes in the ice," Joe said.

"Large enough to stash a bag of stolen loot under the ice," Frank said.

Hank and Ray looked at Frank in disbelief.

"You think Ernie and those kids are stealing the stuff, hiding it in the lake, and marking the spots with tinfoil?" Hank asked.

"I'm not sure about Ernie," Frank admitted hesitantly.

"Works for me," Joe said. "Let's check it out."

"All right, we need some gear," Frank said.

"Does that mean we're done fishing?" Ray asked.

"Yeah, sure," Joe said. "But we may need you later if you're not busy."

"I'm all yours," Ray said.

"Me, too," said Hank.

"All right, we'll call you," Frank said.

Frank and Joe's first call was to Phil Cohen. "Phil, we're going to need a metal detector, your map, and the GPS."

Then Frank called Officer Riley and asked him to stop by the lake later because they might have some evidence for him. Then he called Hank and Ray and arranged to meet them at the Kwans' house.

By the time Frank and Joe pulled into Phil's driveway, it was already getting dark.

"I think I've got everything," Phil said. He climbed into the back of the van with his GPS, a metal detector, an ax, and an ice pick.

"Phil, you don't need to come along. This could be dangerous," Frank said.

"I wouldn't miss it for the world," Phil replied.

Hank and Ray were already at the Kwans' house when the Hardys arrived with Phil.

"Do you need more help?" Mr. Kwan asked.

"I think we've got everything covered," Frank said. "Besides, just letting us use your place is help enough."

"So what's the plan?" Ray asked.

"Joe and Ray, you'll keep an eye on Ernie's. If it looks like they're onto us, give us a signal," Frank said.

"Two short whistles and a long one," Joe said.

"We'll give you ten minutes to get into position," Frank said.

Joe and Ray took off for Ernie's. They ran through the woods so they'd be hidden. When they reached Tuttle's, they could see lights on inside, but they didn't dare get too close and risk being seen. Joe's big concern was that the Tuttles might hear Frank and the others chipping at the ice. They decided to split up to watch both entrances to the shop.

After giving Joe and Ray time to get in position, Frank, Phil, and Hank made their way out onto the lake. It was a cold, crisp night.

"I was hoping it would be cloudy," Frank said as he looked at the moonlit lake.

"Where's Riley?" Phil asked.

"I'm sure he's on the way," Frank said. "I just hope we have something to show him when he gets here."

"I'll lead the way," Hank said as he pressed at the ice with a long stick. "None of you know this ice like I do."

Phil followed along, watching the greenish glow of the LCD screen on the GPS unit.

"Over here, to the right," Phil said as he checked the GPS reading against Joe's list of locations.

"This is it," Phil said. He put the GPS in his pocket and turned on the metal detector. He put the headphones on and waved the detector gently over the ice and snow, covering a few square yards before he suddenly stopped.

"Right here," he proclaimed.

Frank got down on his hands and knees and swept the snow away from under the metal detector. The ice underneath was mottled white. Hank started chipping away at it with the ax, trying to be quiet. The sound echoed across the lake.

Frank and Hank cut through five inches of ice before they came to a ball of tinfoil.

"What are we looking for?" Hank asked.

"My guess is that there's fishing line around here somewhere," Frank said.

He used the ice pick to scratch away at the ice around the ball of foil.

"Anything?" Phil asked.

Frank took off his gloves and gently tried to lift the ball of foil from the ice. As it began to pull apart, he felt a slight tug and saw a bit of clear fishing line attached to it.

"There's the fishing line. Give me the ax," Frank said.

He chipped away at the ice around the fishing line. But he stopped short when he heard Joe's signal, two short whistles followed by a long one.

Joe was watching the flickering light of a television against the window of Tuttle's back room when he saw two dark figures come out of the front of the bait shop.

"It's Stu and Neil," Joe whispered to the night air.

"What'll we do?" Ray whispered back.

"What are you doing *here?*" Joe asked, his temper rising.

"I got bored back there—so what? Now, what are we going to do?" repeated Ray.

Joe didn't have time to clobber Ray for leaving his post. "We'll try to buy some time," Joe said as he walked out of the shadows toward the bait shop. "Hey, Neil, Stu, over here."

Rather than respond to his call, Neil and Stu ran behind the shop. Joe heard the unmistakable roar of an engine. Then he saw Stu and Neil take off toward the lake on a snowmobile.

Frank, Hank, and Phil had chipped the ice away

from the fishing line and were pulling the line up from the icy water when they heard the roar of the snowmobile.

"What's that?" Phil asked.

"Kill the flashlights," Frank said.

Phil and Hank turned off their flashlights, but their dark outlines on the white ice stood out in the moonlight.

Frank wasn't going to leave the lake until he found the loot. He kept pulling on the fishing line and found it was attached to a piece of heavy rope. He frantically hauled in the rope as he heard the roar of the snowmobile engine coming closer.

"Do you see anything?" Hank asked.

"We have to get out of here," Phil said, looking toward the sound of the revving engine.

Frank pulled the rope up and a dark plastic bag came to the surface. He opened the bag and saw a sparkle of silver gleaming in the moonlight.

"Bingo," Frank said, scrambling to get the bag out of the water.

"Frank, come on," Phil said as he began to run. The snowmobile was getting closer. Hank was already halfway to the Kwans' house.

The roar of the engine grew louder, and the ice began to shake. Then the ice began to shudder. Frank felt what was coming. Dragging his booty behind him, he took off a few feet behind Phil and just a few inches in front of the cracking ice.

16 Gotcha!

Frank tried to run as gently as he could, but there was no way to move without causing the ice to splinter around him. The snowmobilers obviously knew what they were doing. They swung around in a wide arc and started straight toward Frank and Phil from solid ice. Frank stood frozen. If he moved, he'd be under the ice in a flash. If he didn't, the snowmobile would crack the rest of the ice and he'd still go under.

But maybe, he thought, they'll go under, too. He took that as his consolation as he braced himself for impact.

At the last moment, the snowmobile swerved away, missing Frank by inches. Frank's resolve had deserted him. He found himself pressed flat on the ice and felt a cold whoosh of air as Stu swung a heavy steel ice bar just above his head.

"Phil, get down," Frank shouted as he watched the snowmobile chase after his friend.

But Phil kept running. Stu swung the ice bar and caught him behind his knees, which sent him sprawling.

Frank tried to spread his body out as far as possible along the cold, cracking ice. If I can distribute my weight over a greater area, he thought, I might not break through. The noise of ice breaking up seemed to surround him as he waited for Stu and Neil to return for him.

Frank finally lifted his head to see how close they were and was surprised to see two figures on ice skates chasing after the snowmobile.

As he watched in astonishment, one of the skaters peeled off and skated over to him. It was Joe!

"Don't come any closer! The ice is breaking up," Frank shouted to his brother. "Back there." Frank tried to nod his head backward. "Get the metal detector."

Joe skated past Frank and swooped down, grabbing the long handle of the metal detector.

"What am I supposed to do with this?" Joe asked.

"Do you remember jousting from history?" Frank responded.

"I would have paid more attention in class if I'd known it would come to this," Joe said.

He maneuvered the long handle of the metal detector so he could use it as a lance, thrusting it out a few feet in front of them.

"Don't fall through the ice while I'm gone," Joe told his brother.

"Wouldn't think of it," Frank replied. "Now, *charge!*"

Neil and Stu turned and came back at Frank and Joe, with Ray trailing behind them on his skates. Stu had the heavy ice bar sticking out a few feet on the right side.

"Go for the right," Frank said. Joe pushed off and sprinted straight toward his opponent.

Joe's push-off caused the ice around Frank to break up a little more. He felt as if he was floating on a number of tiny frozen islands, but he was still on top of, not under, the water.

Frank watched the dark outline of his brother spin around as the snowmobile buzzed him. Joe's stab with the metal detector had no effect. But Stu and Neil seemed to catch on to the game. They made a wide arc and started for Joe with ferocious speed.

Frank couldn't watch this time as his brother took off to confront the snowmobile. He focused on the crack that ran through the ice just below his nose. All he heard was a war cry from Joe and the sound of metal against metal. Then all was almost silent, except for the sound of the snowmobile coming closer and closer. He couldn't help but raise his head.

Before he could even shut his eyes, the snowmobile was upon him. Frank expected to be dead, but he curiously still felt alive—cold, wet, but alive. The air was silent for a moment, and then suddenly thunder roared in Frank's ears. He looked up, right before he went under, to see the snowmobile disappearing under the ice, with Stu and Neil trying to use each other as a ladder to get out.

"Help me! Help!" Neil called out as he flailed in the icy water.

Joe grabbed the rope that was tied around the sack of stolen loot Frank had been hauling and carefully approached the hole where Neil, Stu, the snowmobile, and Frank had fallen through.

"Grab the rope," Joe called as he tossed one end of the line.

"Hey, you idiot!" Neil screamed. "I'm over here! Help!"

Frank thrashed in the darkness but missed the rope. Joe threw it again, and this time Frank caught it.

Joe didn't trust that the ice near Frank would hold him, so he tied the rope around his waist and crawled away from the hole on all fours until he felt secure enough to stand.

He took a large breath in through his nose and let it out through his mouth. Then he dug one blade of his skates into the frozen lake and gently, but with all the strength he had, he pushed off. It was a slow process, and Joe did not look back. Stop, breathe, push. Stop, breathe, push. On his fourth go, he felt something give. He didn't know whether it was his back or the ice, but he put all his effort into one last push—and went sailing across the ice.

Horrified he'd lost Frank, he turned and sped back toward the hole. The moonlight had dimmed behind a cloud. The lake looked solid black. Joe raced as fast as he could when suddenly he hit something and went flying. He landed flat on his back, but on solid ice.

"Oh," he moaned. The clouds separated, and in the growing moonlight Joe saw what had tripped him. The long body of Frank Hardy lay on the ice, not moving.

"Frank!" he yelled, and pulled his bruised body up and got it moving.

He knelt beside his brother. "Frank?" he shouted. "Frank!"

Frank opened one chilled eyelid and then the other. Through his shivering blue lips, he said, "I'm cold."

"Hey!" Joe called to the crowd that had gathered to pull Stu and Neil from the lake. "I need help with Frank! Bring blankets! Get a sled!"

Ten minutes later Frank was being carried into the Kwans' house by Con Riley and a paramedic. They had arrived on the scene just as the snowmobile had gone under. Stu and Neil had been saved. Mrs. Kwan had her hands full for the next few hours warming the three icemen, inside and out.

In front of the roaring fire, Joe and Officer Riley stood warming themselves.

"Stu and Neil Tuttle are your robbers," Frank said to Officer Riley. "They've been stashing the stuff in the lake under the ice."

"Well, they won't be going anywhere for a while now, and when they do, it'll be in handcuffs," Riley promised.

Phil hobbled in, held upright by Ray Nelson.

"Where have you two been?" Riley asked.

"I kept running after that creep clipped me with his steel bar—" Phil began.

"Neil, or was it Stu? One of those two jerks," Joe informed the officer.

"I saw him running," Ray said. "I knew he wouldn't get far with his legs so bruised. I could tell they were already starting to buckle, so I went after him."

"Good thing, too," Phil said with a smile. "Next thing I knew, I was being dragged through the woods on some kind of handmade stretcher, pulled by this guy." He pointed at his crutch, Ray, and smiled broadly.

"So, here we are. End of story," Ray finished the short tale.

"Not quite, Ray Nelson," Phil said. "I'd have died of exposure out there if no one had come after me. You can't deny it, Ray—you did something good."

"Yeah, well, don't spread it around," Ray said. "I have a reputation to protect."

Riley took Phil up to the bedroom where the paramedic and Mrs. Kwan were taking care of one of the other injured parties.

Ray took a seat near the fire.

"So, you did something good," Joe said with a hint of anger in his voice. "Well, how about explaining to me why you left your post at the bait shop so those two could get to their snowmobile?"

Ray seemed to get a bit defensive. "Look, Joe, you're a Hardy. A golden boy. Always a hero. So maybe I'm no courageous detective like you, okay?

I figured if those two came out back, I'd be toast. It wouldn't be a fair fight."

"But you let them take the snowmobile and almost kill my brother, not to mention Phil. They'd have gotten us, too, you know," Joe countered.

"Let me finish," Ray said. "I didn't want to fight them, just me against them, so I drained the gasoline from their snowmobile and went back to join you."

Joe's mouth dropped open. "You what?" A hint of a smile began to creep onto his face. "You *what?*"

"Why else did you think they suddenly stopped before they could bean your brother? Why else did they let the snowmobile stop on thin ice? They were out of gas!"

Joe felt like hugging Ray, but instead, he walked over to him and shook his hand.

"Aw, c'mon," Ray complained. "I'm a hero, too, now!"

They gave each other big football-player hugs, hooting and shouting, "Victory!"

Soon all the invalids—the perpetrators and the victims alike—were seated by the fire, drinking hot chocolate and swapping stories of their near-death experiences. But Con Riley kept a close eye on Neil and Stu Tuttle.

When Mrs. Kwan and the paramedic gave the okay, the party broke up. Officer Riley slapped handcuffs on the Tuttles, and everyone went out to see them off in the squad car.

Just as Stu and Neil were about to duck their heads to get into the car, Ernie Tuttle drove up.

"What's going on here?" Ernie shouted.

"That's what I'd like to ask you," Riley said. "What do you know about these boys and those robberies?" Riley asked as he grabbed Stu and Neil and made them face Ernie.

"Stu, Neil, what are they doing to you?" Ernie demanded.

"These two have been doing some breaking and entering on their visits, and hiding the loot in the lake," Officer Riley said.

Ernie looked at Stu in disbelief. "Stu, is this true?"

Stu turned away from his grandfather without speaking.

"Neil?"

Neil hung his head.

"I don't believe it," Ernie kept muttering. But from the looks on his grandsons' faces, Ernie knew it was true.

A few days later the Kwans threw a celebration party.

Once again Frank and Joe drove a vanload of their friends around the last bend in the road and saw the postcard panorama of the frozen lake, but the ice-fishing shantytown at the one end showed no signs of fishermen, and there were no hockey players at the other end. They had been the first guests to arrive at the party, though they stayed on opposite ends of the living room.

"Hey, it's hot back here. Can you open a window?" Callie called from the backseat.

"Complain to Phil. He's the one who fixed the heat," Frank called back.

"There's no pleasing some people," Joe said with a laugh.

Even Ray's dad had decided to come to the party, since he was sure Ernie wouldn't show up.

Frank and Joe were standing by the fireplace when Chief Collig arrived.

"I have to thank you boys for cracking the case," Collig said. The rest of the guests applauded.

"Thanks," Frank said. "But we couldn't have done it without the help of most of you in this room."

"Especially the medical care provided by our hostess," Joe said, waving to Mrs. Kwan.

Just as the fishermen were beginning to talk to Ray and his friends, Ernie Tuttle came in the front door.

"Excuse me," Ernie said awkwardly. "I don't mean to barge in. I just wanted to say I'm sorry about all the trouble my grandsons caused. I feel terrible about what's been going on. If I'd had any idea, I would have straightened those boys out."

"They'll get their due in jail," Chief Collig said.

Ernie looked around the room and saw Ray and his dad.

"I've also got to say a special apology to Ray Nelson," Ernie said. There was a general gasp among the crowd. "Ray, I'm sorry I blamed you. I know you're a wiseguy, but it was wrong of me to accuse you of anything worse."

Ray came across the room and, much to Ernie's

surprise, reached out to shake his hand. "It's okay, Ernie."

The awkward silence that followed was broken as Ray's father made his way through the crowd. "Excuse me . . . excuse me."

Ray's dad walked up to Ernie with his hand outstretched. "Ernie, we can go on hating each other if you want, but let's not drag everyone else into our troubles," Mr. Nelson said. The guests clearly could not believe what was happening.

The two men shook hands and the whole room erupted into cheers and applause.

"The truth is," Ernie said, "I think maybe the reason the fishing is so good at my end of the lake is all the noise you boys cause at the other end with your hockey games. You scare all the fish right to my front door," Ernie said as the fishermen started laughing.

"Maybe you should pay us to play hockey," Ray said.

Chief Collig put his arm around Ray's shoulder. "I don't know about paying you, but there is the matter of your breaking into one of those houses. I know how much you like working on cars, so I'll expect you to spend every Saturday for the next two months down at the police station tuning up police cruisers."

Ray looked as though he'd just won the lottery. "Really? That's great."

Everyone relaxed and returned to their conversations and hot cider and chocolate.

"Hey, Hardys, who's up for a game of hockey?" Ray cried.

146

"You boys serious about learning to ice-fish?" Ernie asked Frank and Joe.

"What about that speed race the two of you were going to have?" Callie asked.

Frank and Joe just waved the lot of them off and sat by the fire until it was time to go home.

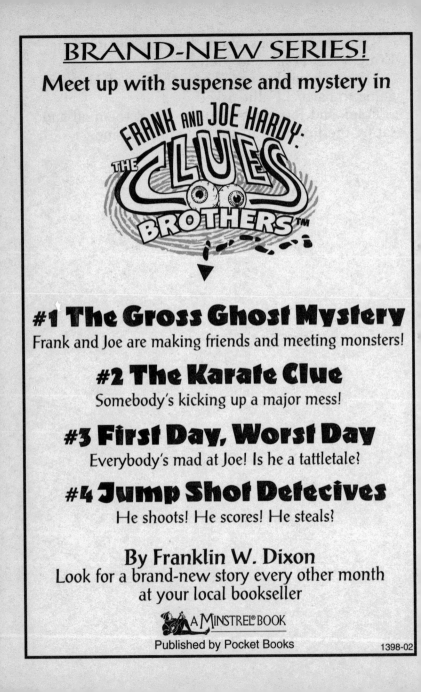